COMPASS BOX KILLER

Piyush Jha is an acclaimed film director, ad filmmaker and the author of the bestselling novel, *Mumbaistan*.

A student political leader at university, he pursued a career in advertising management after acquiring an MBA degree. Later, he switched tracks, first to make commercials for some of the country's largest brands, and then to write and direct feature films. His films include *Chalo America*, *King of Bollywood* and *Sikandar*.

He lives in his beloved Mumbai, where he can often be found walking the streets that inspire his stories.

Praise for *Mumbaistan*

'[*Mumbaistan*] is as pulpy as they come and fans of the genre may even find it un-put-downable. A definite read for those looking for thrilling page-turners.'   —*DNA*

'The book starts off guns ablaze and manages [to] maintain a constant intensity.'   —*TimeOut Mumbai*

'The stories are cut by scenes with precision, making sure that the pace never falters.'   —*The Hindu*

'*Mumbaistan* [is] a crime thriller novel that explores the gritty underbelly of Mumbai in a compelling, powerful manner.'
—*Society*

'This will keep you engrossed through a flight or a train journey.'
—*Sunday Mid-Day*

'*Mumbaistan* is certainly the most appropriate city crime-noir, the ready-to-go variety that promises to keep you at the edge of your seat. A page-turner in the truest sense.'   —*The Hitavada*

'The plots seem simple enough on the surface but each ends with a "twist in the tale."'   —*The Statesman*

'Jha is a deft raconteur who knows how to keep his audiences (call them readers) engrossed in the twists and turns with which he imbues all his tales.'   —*The Sunday Tribune*

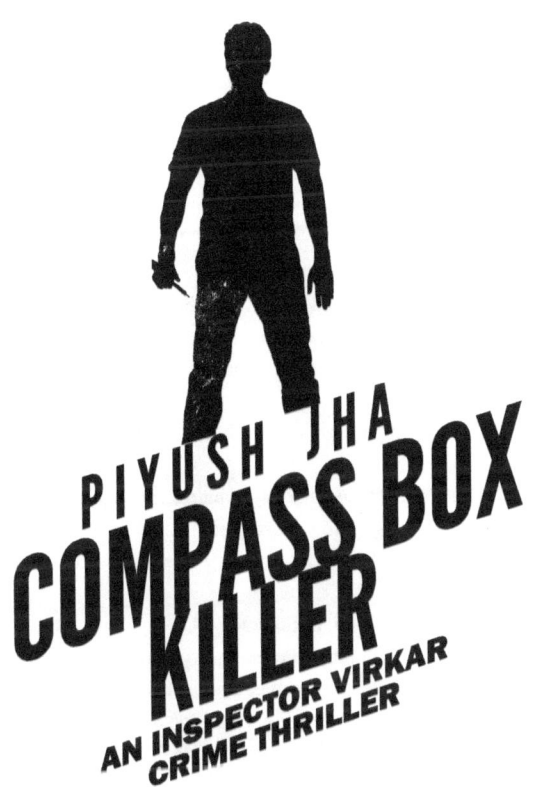

PIYUSH JHA

COMPASS BOX KILLER

AN INSPECTOR VIRKAR CRIME THRILLER

RUPA

Published by
Rupa Publications India Pvt. Ltd 2013
7/16, Ansari Road, Daryaganj
New Delhi 110002

Sales centres:
Allahabad Bengaluru Chennai
Hyderabad Jaipur Kathmandu
Kolkata Mumbai

ISBN: 978-81-291-2427-2

10 9 8 7 6 5 4 3 2 1

The moral right of the author has been asserted.

To my wife Priyanka,

whose continued belief in me is my greatest strength.

Prologue

His hands were clasped around her throat. It hurt, but it *so* turned her on. The feeling was not entirely new to her—the pleasure of pain. The two times that they had been together before, he had pleasured her with it. Now, as he rubbed himself urgently against her body, she could feel him ready to oblige her again.

Today, though, things had moved so fast that she only just realized that they were still standing at the threshold of the door to her room. 'Come with me,' she whispered, tugging at his hands around her throat. He let his hands fall. Holding his left hand while taking a few tentative steps backwards, she pulled him towards the huge bathroom attached to the plush guest room of the sprawling bungalow. Once inside, she stepped towards the edge of the large bathtub that was already three-quarters full of foaming warm water.

When the Smooth Operator had knocked on her door a few minutes ago, she had been running a bath, waiting to soak herself in it. He had stepped inside and, without a word, enveloped her in his strong arms. She had responded to his soft, sensuous kiss more out of instinct than desire. He had taken this response as carte blanche and proceeded to fondle her breasts that were no longer fettered by the bra she had discarded on the bathroom floor. Protected only by a thin layer of the soft silk bathrobe she had hurriedly pulled on to answer the door, she had responded quickly to his touch. He had pushed apart the folds of her silk gown to let her breasts feel the slight nip in the November evening air in Khandala. Then, he had slid his tongue across her breasts to fully electrify her body into submission. The soft moan that had escaped from her lips had been a signal for his hands to move downwards, to the flat of her stomach. She had not allowed him to go lower, however, clasping her legs together and blocking his eager fingers. This was not because she didn't want him, but because she was still enjoying his ministrations on her breasts. Soon, he had grown impatient. He wanted more. His greedy mouth had rapidly moved from one breast to the other and he had snaked his hands up to her throat, stroking it gently with his thumbs. She had moaned again. Suddenly, his tongue had turned rough, his hands tightening their grasp around her neck. A raw excitement had taken over her. She stopped resisting and had egged him on with her aroused shivers.

Now, as they reached the edge of the bathtub, she motioned for him to step into the water that was now overflowing with bubbles from the bubble-bath liquid she had poured in earlier. He took charge again, reaching for her bathrobe and peeling it off in one smooth motion until she stood naked. Growing wet with anticipation as he tore the clothes off his own body, she sank into the frothy water until nothing but her head could be seen rising out of the bubbles. He, too, lowered himself into the foam, sitting across from her. Spreading his legs across her slippery thighs, he interlocked them behind her back, pulling her close to him and pressed his lips against hers. As his tongue thrust into her mouth, she felt the now-familiar slide of his hands to her naked neck—but this time, his grip was tighter. Feeling slightly uncomfortable with his tightening chokehold, she squirmed a little, indicating that she wanted him to ease up, but realized that he was in no mood to let go. In an attempt to distract him, she reached out and stroked him underwater, only to discover that he was getting harder and harder with every little squeeze of her neck. Finding it difficult to breathe now, she tried to push him away but he seemed to get more aroused by this. He squeezed her neck harder and pressed himself against her.

Her body began to struggle, seeking release from his unyielding grip. She wanted to scream but no sound came out of her throat. Down below in the water, she could feel him between her legs, probing urgently, entering her. Her whole body thrashed against him in an effort to escape, but this only made him more frenzied as he continued to thrust himself roughly into her.

Suddenly, all energy drained from her body. Her limbs slackened and a black fog began to envelope her brain, dulling every painful sensation. Yet she was alert enough to recognize that the blackness spelt danger. Should she succumb to it, she would not see the brightness of another day.

Fear took control of her now; it gave her the strength she didn't think she had. But she also knew that the adrenaline wouldn't last long. In a last-ditch effort, her left hand broke free from his clutches and clattered against the side of the bathtub. *She had to escape*. Her fingertips grazed against her rumpled pair of jeans lying discarded on the floor. She felt something hard in its pocket. *Cell phone*, her brain screamed in recognition from the recesses of her foggy mind. She shifted her position with difficulty, continuing to feel his savage attack below the water. Deep down inside, she knew she was fighting a losing battle. Her fingers brushed against the keypad of the cell phone, feeling the shape of the letters engraved on each key. She pressed one key, then another. Press…press…press. Finally, the cell phone slipped from her grasp and fell to the floor next to the bathtub even as her fingers continued to press keys in the empty air long after the air in her lungs had died.

The Smooth Operator didn't notice. In fact, he hadn't been aware of anything for the past ten minutes—his mind had switched itself off as he sank deeper and deeper into the throes of ecstasy. The fact that her body had no life left in it made no difference to him in his animal state of arousal. It was only after he was fully spent that he noticed that her eyes had turned within her skull and that all he could see were the whites.

A ragged scream of realization escaped the Smooth Operator's mouth as he finally released her throat and shrank back from her bubble-lathered corpse.

1

Mumbai

The young man, who would soon be known in the media as 'The Compass Box Killer', stood sweating in the sun. Beads of perspiration ran down the dark, exposed skin of his semi-naked shoulders and soaked the ragged, soft cloth of his banian. Some droplets found their way down to the earth, sliding down the thin, dark, almost hairless legs that stuck out of the baggy khaki shorts like cricket stumps. The killer's hawk-like eyes, embedded in his youthful, gaunt face just below his wide forehead, were fixed upon the sign on the single-storey building in front of him: Wamanrao Marg Police Station.

The iconic police station, once known as the Robert Circle Police Station, had been in service since the times of the British. It is from here that police contingents were dispatched to foil the Quit India Movement of 1942. In the post-Independence boom, its strategic location between the areas of Byculla, Mumbai Central and Grant Road had granted it a special status when it came to policing nefarious activities in Mumbai's oldest and most crowded neighbourhoods. It was said that the toughest policemen in Mumbai were posted here, due to whom many a criminal operating in the mean streets of Mumbai was meted out quick justice. Today, however, the police station was going to witness justice of a different kind.

Policemen of all shapes and sizes bustled in and out of the busy police station paying no attention to the young man standing right in front of them. He wasn't a killer yet, but if the policemen could read his mind, they would have made all attempts to stop him in his tracks.

The young man drew in a deep breath and took a few steps forward; no one noticed him as he walked through the arched portals of the old British building into the large office area. From a corner, the blubbering whine of a battered wife seeking justice rose through the air, only to be drowned out by the loud guffaws of two police constables merrily watching their colleagues brutally slap the accused husband. Quick justice was the hallmark of Wamanrao Marg Police Station. The young man ducked into the wide passage that led around the office area. As he walked, his feet fell in step with the steady 'clack-clack' of an ancient typewriter emanating from somewhere deep within the cabins lining the passageway. The angry protests of a prostitute who had been held at the police station through the night could be heard in the background as the young man strode towards a swivel door that led into a large office chamber at the end of the passage. 'Senior Inspector Tukaram Akurle' was emblazoned across the door. An old, tired-looking police constable was dozing off on a wooden bench outside the office. The young man tip-toed up to the door, but the constable didn't make a move, slumping deeper into his afternoon slumber, as was his daily routine. Emboldened, the young man parted the swivel door and entered the empty chamber inside, taking care not to make even the slightest noise.

A huge glass-topped wooden writing table with an overlarge chair dominated the dimly-lit room. A few scrawny metal chairs faced the table in subservience. A fat, naked, 200-watt light bulb hung over the table. Maps dividing the entire Wamanrao Marg area into smaller sections adorned the walls of the room. On the far wall, a red graph tracked the fluctuating fortunes of crime in the area over the past decade. A large, precariously-stacked pile of dusty, crumbling old files and used stationery in the corner behind the table was the only eyesore in the otherwise sparse, neat room.

The young man strode silently up to the dusty pile and pulled out a small, rectangular package wrapped in a newspaper that was bulging from the pocket of his khaki shorts. He bent down and quickly stuffed the package under the lowest file, taking care to hold the pile steady. Although a casual observer would be unable to see the package, the man still pushed at it, trying to shove it away from sight completely.

A sharp voice cut through the air behind him. 'Hey! What are you doing?'

The young man turned his attention to the glass of chai lying at the foot of the glass-topped table beside the pile. Picking it up, he turned to look the source of the voice in the eye.

He ran his fingers through his hair and said, 'Nothing, saheb, I was just collecting your glass, see? It's time for your afternoon chai, right?'

Senior Inspector Akurle smiled at him through his corpulent features. The soft, shapeless mass that was his stomach hung over his uniform belt. It jiggled as he waddled to his desk. 'Yes it is, and make sure that you get me two garam vada paos along with it.'

The young man smiled back. 'With extra lasoon chutney, as usual?'

Akurle's smile widened. 'Yes! You're a smart boy. Only two days on the job and you know my likes and dislikes already. Good!'

The youngster smiled a little self-consciously. 'I'm trying hard, saheb.'

The Inspector sighed, 'If only the rest of my police station was like you.'

The young man fidgeted, not wanting to prolong the conversation. 'I'll be back in just ten minutes.'

Distracted by an important-looking circular lying on his table, Akurle nodded and waved him away. The young man turned and walked out of the swivel door, bobbing his head in obeisance to the now fully-alert constable standing ramrod straight at his post by the door.

A casual whistle found its way to the young man's lips as he walked back through the passageway and out into the street towards the chai stall that stood across the road.

2

Inspector Virkar picked up the glass mug topped-up with Godfather Beer, his favourite. Taking care to not let even a single drop escape its confines, he raised the mug to take a sip when a flickering movement across the dimly-lit room caught his eye.

'Aai cha gho!' a muted curse escaped his lips as his eyes focused on the colourfully-clad figure of a girl in the distance. He put down the mug, casting a single glance of regret at the rapidly disappearing foam atop the liquid and turned his attention back to the girl. Mike in hand, she was just getting into her act on a small, elevated stage set up on the far corner of Lotus Bar. Soon, the first bars of her signature song rose up mellifluously from her garishly painted lips and filled the room with a happy buzz. As was always the case, the girl seemed to have a magical effect on the patrons of Lotus Bar; almost all conversations stopped as lust-filled eyes turned towards her. The girl's lithe body swayed as she sang a song that spoke of joyous times in the days gone by. However, her eyes didn't seem to believe any of the words emanating from her mouth and, although her face displayed a fixed smile, the drooping corners of her mouth reflected an incomprehensible sadness that the bar's patrons barely noticed.

Virkar seemed to be drawn into the song—only a close observer would have seen his gaze shift to the scraggly, middle-aged man sitting a few tables away from him in the darker shadows of the bar. The man returned Virkar's look with a slight nod. Suddenly, rising from his table, he rushed towards the singer shouting, 'Binky...Binky!'

The singer stopped singing, stunned. Her sad eyes locked on to the middle-aged man who was striding towards her through the smoke-filled haze of the bar. They lit up with recognition. Happiness shone on her face for the first time since taking the mike. 'Papa!'

The single word rang out through the mike like a shrill announcement. Lotus Bar's waiters and patrons watched in shock as the bizarre scenario unfolded in front of them. As the middle-aged man reached the stage, the girl dropped the mike and rushed towards him. He opened his arms and she sprang into them with a squeal of repressed joy. 'Binky...my daughter, I've found you at last!' The man's delight was audible to everyone in the room.

Virkar rose from his seat and walked towards the father and daughter and suddenly, the spell broke. Tough-looking bouncers surrounded the middle-aged man and Binky and began to pull them apart.

'Thamba!' Virkar barked, his deep, bass-endowed voice cutting through the commotion. The words were spoken with just the right amount of intimidating force, one that could only be used by a man of the law. The bouncers froze and looked towards him with respect. For a few seconds, Virkar stared them down, his lean, muscular body poised for a fight. Then he began to walk towards them, the way he moved clearly conveying that he had participated in many a street brawl and won. But what really made the bouncers shrink back was the fact that, even in the smoke-filled room, Virkar's eyes were clear—clear to the point of being expressionless—almost as if he didn't care how much damage he inflicted on anyone who didn't follow his orders. Virkar smiled to himself. He could always rely on his powerful voice and carriage to create an impact.

'What's going on here?' he demanded.

'She is my daughter, saheb. I have been looking for her for three years,' the middle-aged man blurted out.

Virkar looked pointedly at the singer. 'Tell me, is this true?'

Despite Virkar's aggressive, no-nonsense tone, Binky cast a nervous glance at the burly bouncers.

Virkar voice turned gentle. 'Don't be afraid. I am a police officer.'

The change of tone had its desired effect and Binky burst into tears. Falling at the middle-aged man's feet, she began to wail. 'Please forgive me, papa. I was wrong to run away from home. Take me back, take me away from here!'

A man dressed in a cheap black jacket stepped up. 'You can't leave right now. You have a contract with us,' he said, his tone threatening.

Virkar ignored the man. 'How old are you?' he asked Binky.

'Sixteen,' piped up the middle-aged man.

'That's a lie! She's eighteen as per our records,' retorted the man in the black jacket who, by now, had started to sweat.

'Okay. Go and get your records,' said Virkar without hesitation.

Black Jacket lost all his bravado and fell into a sullen silence.

'I will have to take these two with me to the police station to record their statement,' Virkar announced loudly to no one in particular. But before he could say anything else, a dark, portly man in an electric blue silk lungi-kurta ensemble emerged from the door behind the stage. Everyone except Virkar and the father-daughter duo moved aside in deference as he sauntered forward. The chunky gold chains around his neck and wrists shone under the bright lights of the stage. His thick, bushy moustache hung over even thicker lips which parted lazily to ask, 'Why are you getting involved in this, Inspector Virkar saheb?' As a Lotus Bar regular, Virkar recognized the man as Sadhu Anna, the owner.

Sadhu Anna continued, 'These kind of things happen daily in our business, saheb. Please take your seat and I'll send you another beer. Or better still, I've just received a couple of cases of your favourite Godfather Beer from Delhi; I'll send them to your home. Enjoy!'

'This is a serious matter, Anna. This girl is underage,' said Virkar, without backing down.

Sadhu Anna raised his portly, gold-laden arm and placed it around Virkar's shoulders. He smirked. 'Virkar, nothing is going to come out of this. You know all your seniors are my friends, don't you?'

Virkar's eyes turned to steel. 'You're right, Sadhu Anna. So, maybe I should get a few of the juniors who are my friends to start questioning all these nice customers sitting in your bar to check whether they have liquor permits,' he replied in a loud voice that carried across the bar. Immediately, a few patrons slammed down whatever money they had in their pockets and quickly slunk towards the door. Virkar was amused to see Sadhu Anna's mounting irritation.

He turned to Virkar. 'Why are you behaving like a filmy hero?'

Virkar shrugged. 'This is a filmy situation. A father goes to a bar for a drink and finds the daughter he had lost, performing there. But the villainous bar owner does not let them reunite. A policeman, who is also at the bar, comes to their rescue. The villainous bar owner lets them go with the policeman because he realizes that the policeman will otherwise make his life a living hell.'

Sadhu Anna spat on the floor of the stage. 'All right, take them with you. But remember, you will no longer be welcome here. And I will be speaking to your seniors.'

Without wasting another second, Virkar held Binky's wrist with one hand, her father's with the other and pulled them towards the exit. Sadhu Anna watched them for a few tense moments and then turned towards the bouncers and waiters. 'Laudu log, what are you all staring at me for? Get the next singer!' he yelled.

Outside the Lotus Bar, Virkar hailed a cab. He made the father and daughter sit in the back seat while himself getting into the front. 'Girgaon Police Station,' he told the driver.

No one spoke a word during the ride. The father and daughter sat in tense silence. The cab had only driven for about ten minutes before stopping at the signal in front of Mumbai Central Railway Station when Virkar handed the surprised cab driver a hundred rupee note.

'Change rakhle,' he patted the driver and waved him away.

Virkar asked his co-passengers to get out of the cab. Then, reaching into his pocket, Virkar fished out two train tickets and handed them to the middle-aged man who was overcome with emotion. 'I will never forget your good deed, Inspector Virkar. Thank you,' he said.

Binky joined her hands in namaste, too choked for words.

Virkar cleared his throat and pointed towards the railway station. 'You'd better hurry. Your train leaves in fifteen minutes.'

The man reached out and hugged Virkar. Turning to his daughter, he said, 'Seek his blessings; he is like God for us.' She immediately bent down to touch Virkar's feet as a sign of respect.

Embarrassed, Virkar took a step back. 'Please go…before I change my mind and take you to the police station.'

The man's eyes flew to Virkar's face in panic but relaxed when he noticed the smile twitching at the corners of the Inspector's mouth. He motioned to Binky and together they rushed towards the railway station's gate.

Like an anxious parent, Virkar watched them merge with the crowd. Only after they had disappeared from sight did his thoughts go back to when he had spotted Binky's grainy picture while reading the Sunday edition of *The Hitavada* (a habit he had picked up from his days in the Gadchiroli district of interior Maharashtra). Binky had been lucky that Virkar, probably the only policeman in Mumbai who read *The Hitavada*, also frequented the bar that she had been semi-sold to. All her dreams of becoming a famous singer in Bollywood had come crashing down on to the stage floor of Lotus Bar. Virkar's trained eye had picked up the fact that the garishly made-up singer he listened to every other night was the same Binky who had disappeared from her home in Bhopal a few months ago. Years of experience had also made Virkar aware that Lotus Bar's owner Sadhu Anna's connections within the police were so strong that, should Virkar have pursued the case officially, his efforts would surely have been tied up in red tape and consigned to a dusty back shelf of a storeroom full of unsolved cases. As for the underaged Binky, she would have been shuttled from one juvenile remand home to another for 'protection' until the paperwork was done, and after having been satisfactorily ravished by corrupt, lecherous officials, she would finally be spat out on to the streets of Mumbai with no choice but to sell her soul to feed her already ravaged body. After some amount of rumination, Virkar had called Binky's father on the number listed in the advertisement with a plan.

Virkar walked towards the parking lot of the railway station to extricate his Bullet motorcycle from the jumbled mass of two-wheelers. He had parked it there earlier in the evening when he had bought the rail tickets. As he kicked the Bullet to a start, the only regret that Virkar had was that his days frequenting the Lotus Bar were over—it was one of the few bars in Mumbai that served Godfather Beer. 'Khao, khujao, batti bujhao,' he smiled and shrugged, wearing his helmet.

His cell phone rang just as he was about to drive into the traffic. Cursing under his breath, he quickly extricated the phone from his pocket, half-expecting it to be Binky's father. It was his boss, ACP Wagh of the Crime Branch Murder Squad. Before Virkar could say anything, his boss's familiar gravelly voice barked out loud and clear, 'Virkar, report to Wamanrao Marg Police Station immediately. Senior Inspector Akurle has been found dead in his cabin.'

3

Dark clouds rumbled in the Mumbai sky as Virkar stepped into the now sombre-looking Wamanrao Marg Police Station. A constable on duty gave him a sleepy salute and ushered him in. Taking care not to get cornered by the few reporters hanging around, Virkar ducked quickly into the crowded passageway leading to the Senior Inspector's cabin. His long strides came to an abrupt halt, however, when he heard a woman's muted sobs coming from one of the typist's rooms on the side of the passage. At first glance, he couldn't see anything clearly in the semi-darkened room, but as he craned his neck and focused his eyes past the line of old manual typewriters, he saw the huddled figure of a middle-aged woman sitting in the shadows. A female police inspector was doing her best to console her. Virkar surmised that the woman must be Akurle's wife. He stepped into the doorway and cleared his throat, seeking permission to enter. The woman looked at him with wet, anguished eyes.

'Mrs Akurle?' he asked.

The woman sighed and nodded.

Inflecting his voice with the correct amount of sympathy, Virkar continued, 'I'm very sorry to hear about Akurle saheb.'

He pulled up a chair next to hers.

She wiped her eyes with the pallu of her sari. 'I told him so many times to stay away from street-side vada paos. The oil is always stale. But he wouldn't listen.'

Virkar looked at her, nonplussed. 'Vada paos?'

'Yes,' she said, sniffing. 'This morning he woke up with a high fever and started to vomit. He said it was because of the extra peg of scotch he drank last night...' Mrs Akurle trailed off, dabbed her eyes again and continued, '...but I knew it was the vada paos. I told him to go to the hospital but he just wouldn't listen.' Tears welled up again in her eyes. Virkar swallowed hard, a little ashamed of his own addiction to street-side vada paos. His stomach churned involuntarily. 'It's just the beer,' he told himself, hoping that the vada paos he had had for breakfast had been digested by now. He turned his attention back to the weeping woman. 'Have faith in God, vahini. He will give you strength,' Virkar said, bending down and touching her feet as a mark of respect.

He rose and exited the room into the passageway, making his way to the swivel doors through the growing crowd of policemen. He noticed that many of them had covered their noses. Only then did the strong stench of vomit hit him—he had been too preoccupied to notice it earlier. Reeling, he bravely stepped inside Akurle's cabin. The sight made his stomach heave again, this time so violently that the beer in his belly rose to his throat. Clamping his hand over his mouth and nose, he turned his full attention to what lay before him.

Senior Inspector Akurle was seated in his oversized chair, his upper body sprawled across his desk as if he was taking a nap, except for the fact that his eyes were wide open. His mouth was gaping and the contents of his stomach were spread across the glass top of his table in a smelly, slushy, dirt-coloured paste. Mrs. Akurle had been right: small bits of semi-digested vada pao were spread generously in the slushy vomit along with flecks of blood.

As he had been informed by ACP Wagh, the station's Police Inspector in charge of crime (PI Crime), a sub-inspector from the detection unit and a government doctor were waiting for him inside. The sub-inspector saluted Virkar while the PI Crime picked his teeth with a steel paper clip that had been straightened to reach the deep recesses of his mouth. Virkar ignored him. The government doctor looked up at Virkar and said something that was muffled by his white surgical mask—all he could make out was 'food poisoning'. Virkar raised a curious eyebrow and said, 'I've never seen such a severe case of food poisoning.' The government doctor now took off his mask and spoke in a tone that bordered on condescension, 'It happens. It's because of the spurious oil used for frying the vada paos.' The PI Crime added with a bored expression, 'I have taken the vadapaowala into custody. He was using spurious palmolein oil. I have already sent it to the forensic lab for testing.'

Virkar nodded distractedly as he let his eyes wander over the crime scene. 'Glad to see that you've talked to Mrs Akurle and reached a quick conclusion based on what she said. I'm sure she will be happy.' The sub-inspector nodded with pride while Virkar continued, his voice dripping with sarcasm, 'Maybe you should also consider my point of view. I would like to put forth, for your consideration, the proposition that it was not food poisoning. Instead, in my humble opinion, some kind of poison was mixed in his food.'

The PI Crime opened his mouth to protest but Virkar silenced him by raising his hand. 'If it *was* the spurious oil used in the vada pao, we would have received other complaints of food poisoning by now,' he explained, letting the penny drop slowly.

The government doctor looked sheepish but didn't back down. 'Inspector Virkar, I have examined the vomit and found an unknown oily substance mixed with the vada pao...'

'Don't just accept the first possibility because of emotional reasons or because it's easy to explain,' Virkar cut him off. 'Or for the sake of the cameras outside. Please go to your hospital and examine this oily substance thoroughly.' The government doctor didn't argue further and left, looking a few inches shorter than his earlier pompous self. Virkar, ignored the PI Crime and the sub-inspector who hung around fidgeting, and walked towards the pile of old files and stationery beside the glass-topped table. 'What is this?' he asked with a jerk of his head.

'Akurle saheb was in the process of clearing out all the old, unnecessary things in his office,' said the sub-inspector.

Virkar picked up some dusty files and leafed through the sheaf of yellowed papers inside. The dust released by the ruffling of the papers tickled his nose, however, and a loud sneeze rose from him, shooting out into the musty air. The file slipped from Virkar's hands and dropped back on to the pile, kicking up more dust in the process. He instinctively turned away from the pile, but as he did so, a metallic glint caught his eye. After the dust settled, he picked up the files and sifted through them again, this time taking particular care not to release another dust cloud. The object of his attention was lying under the files, partially covered by a crumpled newspaper and glinting in the light of the naked bulb overhead. Virkar bent down and peeled the newspaper away.

It was a student's geometry instrument box. Colloquially known as a 'compass box', this particular one was made of metal, but was so scuffed and battered with age that Virkar could hardly read the brand name stamped on its top. A few dull streaks of paint clung to the compass box's edges, indicating that it might have once been bright yellow ochre in colour. Shrugging, he set it down atop the pile and turned his attention towards the body. He didn't notice that the precariously piled files had teetered under the compass box and were slowly toppling over. All of a sudden, he heard the startled cries of the two other men in the room as a loud crash rang out behind him. The compass box clattered on to the old mosaic tiles and flew open and a piece of paper the size of a visiting card fell out of it. Virkar would not have given it a second glance had he not noticed that the paper had writing on it, and it wasn't in ink. He leaned forward and confirmed his suspicion. The note was written in dried blood. But what was more interesting to Virkar was the message itself: Akurle is just the first to die. To find out who is next, find me first.

4

'Saheb, I beg of you. I don't know anything,' the bleeding, blubbering vadapaowala wailed.

Virkar had just entered the lockup after having spent the night at the government hospital. He hadn't slept a wink and his eyes were bloodshot but his long strides were energetic. He hadn't found the time to take a bath or even change his clothes, so he was still wearing the civvies from last night that now stank of stale cigarette smoke and hospital disinfectant. But he was glad he had personally pushed the government doctor to work through the night to determine the chemical composition of the 'oily substance' found in Akurle's vomit.

'Ricin!' The doctor had finally declared just as the first rays of the sun had lit up the sleeping city. 'He was poisoned with ricin,' he continued, but now he spoke with a mixture of awe and amazement. 'Akurle was fed ricin mixed in the vada paos in such a concentrated dose that it only took a day for the man to die.' Before Virkar could open his mouth, the doctor launched into an explanation in his usual pompous tone, 'Ricin is a little substance that is roughly 1,500 times more toxic than cyanide. Ricin poisoning shuts down the central nervous system and causes multiple organ failure. Its symptoms include fever, nausea, bloody diarrhoea, shock, vomiting, lymph node and kidney damage and, eventually, haemorrhaging and death.'

'So is this ricin readily available in the market?' asked Virkar.

The doctor shook his head. 'No, ricin isn't available by itself, but it can be derived from castor beans which can be easily bought in wholesale subzi mandis across many parts of India. But even then, ricin needs to be extracted from the seeds by a chemical process called chromatography, which takes skill and serious intent.' The doctor sounded thoroughly impressed by the intelligence of the person who had clearly gone to great lengths to plan and commit the murder.

Virkar had driven his Bullet back to the Wamanrao Marg Police Station immediately, allowing himself the single indulgence of taking a detour via Marine Drive. As he rode along the promenade, the cool early morning breeze floating in from the sea had cleared his head. Eager to get the truth out of the vadapaowala, Virkar was armed with the knowledge that the man couldn't have had the scientific know-how that was needed to extract ricin from castor beans.

Now, as he stared into the vadapaowala's terrified eyes, Virkar realized that he was definitely not the killer. The vadapaowala had just been the medium through which the killer had gained access to his target. The man they were looking for was obviously educated and devious enough to have poisoned his victim right under the noses of the best law enforcers of the city. Apart from displaying complete disregard for authority, the killer wanted to engage in some kind of horrific game by sending a message that had sent shivers down the spines of the other policemen at the station.

The police machinery had moved fast. ACP Wagh, in

consultation with his own seniors, had decided to clamp down on the incident fearing a massive uproar in the media. Although Virkar was a new arrival at the Crime Branch, he had been pencilled in as the investigating officer despite others from his department being more experienced and wanting to muscle into a potential high profile case. After being transferred to Mumbai from the Gadchiroli district and serving for only six months at the Colaba police station, Virkar had been transferred to the prestigious Crime Branch. Some said it was because Virkar had political clout. Little known was the fact that his boss in Gadchiroli, Additional Commissioner of Police Abhinav Kumar, was now heading Mumbai's Crime Branch and had personally requested Virkar's transfer to his department. Kumar had observed Virkar closely as the Inspector had valiantly fought the Maoist menace in Gadchiroli at grass-roots level while winning the confidence of the simple tribal folk who had become innocent casualties in the closet war being fought in the jungles. It was Virkar's bravery that had earned him the President's Gallantry Medal, which in turn had secured him a posting in his hometown, Mumbai, and an induction into the elite Murder Squad of the Crime Branch.

ACP Wagh, on the other hand, was eager to ingratiate himself with Abhinav Kumar, which is why he had rooted for Virkar to head the investigation, citing his presence of mind in locating the real clues to the murder before the policemen from Wamanrao Marg Police Station had declared it a case of accidental food poisoning. Virkar had not let on that it was a lucky sneeze that had caught him the break in the case, attributing it to his luck, something he needed very badly to succeed in his new job.

To divert the media's attention, Akurle's death had ironically been attributed to a case of severe gastro-intestinal haemorrhage due to accidental food poisoning. The vadapaowala had been detained in the police station as the unknowing, negligent culprit and was made the media scapegoat—with the tacit understanding that he would be reinstated to his position on the streets at another locality when the heat died down. However, some of the policemen at the station were not satisfied with their prime suspect getting off scot-free. Perhaps it was the fear that they could be the killer's next target or just the anger that wells up in a policeman's heart at an attack on a fellow policeman, but these disgruntled policemen spent the night 'interrogating' the poor vadapaowala to extract whatever little information they could. They subjected him to the infamous 'third degree' through the night until he was close to breaking point—he would have confessed to assassinating Rajiv Gandhi if it meant getting some sort of reprieve from his 'interrogation'.

'Just tell me who made the vada paos,' asked Virkar in a sympathetic tone, looking down at the cowering figure in front of him. The vadapaowala teared up with gratitude, relieved that this lanky police officer with the day-old stubble was not using force to elicit an answer from him. He spoke quickly through his sobs, 'Saheb, I have been frying the vada paos myself for the past ten years. Until today, my delivery boys have never come back with a single complaint.' Virkar's brain quickly processed this piece of information. *That's it! The delivery boy. The innocuous person who no one pays attention to in an office.*

Virkar ran his fingers through his ruffled hair that had not seen a comb in over thirty hours. 'Who delivered the vada pao to Akurle?'

'Saheb, it was that boy, Nandu. A poor young fellow, he had just come from some village near the Karnataka border.'

'Where is this Nandu?'

'He lives somewhere near Kalachowki with some other delivery boys. I just hired him a couple of days ago. He begged me for a job and I took pity on him because he looked like he hadn't eaten in a few days. Plus he spoke Kannada. The Mumbai Central Karnataka Sangha Hostel is close by and many of my customers are Kannadigas, so it always helps if some of us know their language.'

Virkar immediately left the Wamanrao Marg Police Station and made his way to Nandu's address in Kalachowki, taking a few plainclothes policemen with him as backup. Meeting them outside the Jain Derasar on Parel Tank Road, he gave them the description that he had got from the vadapaowala and entered the crowded Bhatwadi Chawl after having placed the plainclothes men in strategic positions to stop Nandu from getting away. However, somewhere deep inside Virkar knew that this was an exercise in futility, because if Nandu were an accomplice of the killer, he would be long gone. On the flip side, if he had merely been used by the killer to deliver the vada paos, Nandu might already be dead, because the seemingly intelligent killer wouldn't have executed such an elaborate plan without having thought of eliminating the only person who could identify him. *Either way, Nandu's living quarters might throw up some vital clues*, thought Virkar.

As he approached the wide-open door of the small room occupied by Nandu and eight others within the crowded tenement, Virkar's fingers brushed against the service revolver at his hip, concealed just under his sweat-stained bush shirt. He wondered if he would need it.

He stepped inside the tenement; it was pitch dark. As his eyes tried to adjust to the gloom, he realized that all around him were prone figures of thin, young men, lying stretched out on the floor. 'Iski maa ka…!' he cursed instinctively, taking them to be unconscious or dead, but soon realized that they were only asleep. The soundness of their sleep indicated that they were probably daily-wage workers who had just returned from pulling a night shift somewhere. Since all the space on the floor was used up by the sleepers, their meagre belongings were wrapped in bundled sheets attached to hooks on the ceiling. Each bundle hung precariously above each sleeper, indicating its ownership. Virkar stood at the door, wondering which one of the sleepers was Nandu, since all of them seemed to match the broad description given to him. One of the young men on the floor opened a curious eye and lazily surveyed him. 'Nandu?' Virkar whispered the question, not wanting to disturb the others.

'Gone,' the half-asleep man whispered back, pointing towards an empty-looking bundle hanging from the ceiling in the far corner of the room. Deciding that he had had enough conversation for the morning, the young man rolled over and went back to sleep. For a second, Virkar felt the urge to join the sleeping men on the floor and shut his fatigued eyes briefly. He sighed, knowing he couldn't do anything like that; instead, he would have to summon the plainclothes policemen to rudely wake up all the men and troop them down to the police station for interrogation. Tip-toeing over the men, he made his way across the room towards the hanging sheet-bundle. As he reached it, he snaked his hand between its folds, searching for anything that might provide some clues of Nandu's whereabouts.

His hand connected with something cold and metallic. Suddenly, his tired brain whirred back to life. Virkar looked at the familiar object grasped in his hand. It was yet another old and battered metal compass box, quite like the first one he had found at the site of Akurle's murder. Virkar gently pried it open with his fingers, his pulse quickening. He was not disappointed; the note screamed at him in blood that seemed fresher than the one on the earlier note: You found me. Now find Dr Prabhat Bhandari.

5

Raashi Hunerwal was angry. She had been waiting for nearly two hours in the visitors' waiting room at the Mumbai Crime Branch headquarters. In the five years of her remarkable career, she had become accustomed to waiting for important people—politicians, businessmen, top guns in the law enforcement hierarchy—but she didn't expect to be kept waiting by someone as inconsequential in the pecking order as this Inspector Virkar. Clad in an expensive-looking pair of stilettos, her impeccably pedicured feet tapped on the floor impatiently. She was thirsty and hungry and desperately wanted to go the washroom, but was controlling herself fearing that the slippery Inspector could use an absence of even five minutes as an excuse to not meet her. He had been avoiding her calls for the past two days but today, Raashi was determined to buttonhole him into spilling the story, strands of which she had picked up from one of her police informants. Something big was happening on the Mumbai crime scene (at least that's what she'd been told) and she was determined to find it, expose it and propel herself into the big leagues of TV journalism. For two years, she had been waiting on the sidelines, diligently digging up dirt on small-time domestic crimes and plastering each sordid little detail of sundry street crimes on her show *Crime Update* on the local CrimeNews channel. She was hankering to take a bite out of the big-time and was waiting to break a story that would score her the massive brownie points she desperately needed to get noticed by the big guns of the national news channels. Today was her day to hit the jackpot, she could feel it.

As the clock passed the two-hour mark, she reached into her patent leather handbag and drew out her compact mirror and lipstick. She flipped open the compact and surveyed her sharp-featured, attractive face for the umpteenth time. Eyes: sky-blue contact lenses. *Check*. Skin: flawless. *Check*. Nose: sharp and straight enough to be called sexy. *Check*. Hair: tightly curled and hanging firmly in place. *Check*. Satisfied, she swiped the lipstick across her full lips, rendered dry by the sultry Mumbai weather and anticipation. Practicing the famous television smile that was known to disarm even the hardest heart, she decided that she was ready, as always, to plunge into her mission. She was going to whip the unsuspecting Inspector Virkar into submission and prove to her colleagues that her nickname, 'Hunterwali', was not unfounded.

Hearing the click of the swivel door of the waiting room, she hastily shoved her compact into her bag. A podgy, oily-haired constable entered the room, a lascivious grin stamped on his face. He looked her up and down; Raashi let his eyes roam over her body, her tight skirt-and-blouse ensemble, until they met her steely gaze. 'Zhala, bhau?' she spat out in Marathi, asking him if he was done leching after her. The shocked constable immediately lowered his gaze with a sudden flush of shame.

'Ma-madam, Virkar saheb is now done with his meeting,' he stammered with embarrassment.

Raashi sprang up without another word and exited through

the swivel door. With the constable shuffling behind her, she briskly walked into the passageway that led to the main office area. Smoothening her skirt, Raashi inhaled sharply before walking through the doors.

She instantly became the cynosure of all the appreciative eyes within the room where officers and other policemen milled about. She avoided all eye contact and marched towards the corner desk that she had earlier identified as Virkar's by slipping a peon a ten-rupee note. As she walked across the large room, the man seated at the desk glanced up from his papers. She took in his clean-cut, unconventionally handsome, swarthy features with some amount of surprise. As he locked his gaze with hers, his dark, sleep-deprived eyes seemed to drill into her with an intensity that sent a ripple of excitement through her. She composed herself and, assuming an aggressive tone that was meant to put Virkar on the defensive, said, 'I'm Raashi Hunerwal from the CrimeNews channel. I've been trying to meet you for two whole days.' Virkar's intense expression turned deadpan. He had been warned about the wily 'Hunterwali' and had secretly been awaiting her arrival. He couldn't help noticing that she was more attractive in person than on TV.

'I've been busy with an investigation,' he shrugged, going back to his papers.

Undeterred, Raashi broke into her trademark smouldering smile. 'Yes, that's what I wanted to speak to you about, Inspector *saheb*—your investigation.' The exaggerated emphasis on 'saheb' was not lost on Virkar.

'Sorry, madam, I have no comments on that,' he said in a businesslike manner.

Raashi calmly pulled up a chair from a nearby desk and sat down. Leaning forward, she enquired in a conspiratorial tone:

'I heard you found another compass box?' Virkar flinched. He was tired and extremely frustrated. He had just spent the last two days interrogating the vadapaowala and Nandu's roommates, and had come up with nothing more than a vague description of the seemingly nondescript young man. The fingerprint experts had not found any prints on the two compass boxes, apart from Virkar's. And, despite all his efforts to keep the details of the case a secret till he had had a breakthrough, someone had leaked information to the media. To make matters worse, Raashi's flirtatious manner, her push-up bra, her soft but too-perfect-to-be-real curls, her artificially luminous eyes and her generously-applied lipstick were only irritating him further. He curbed his urge to question Raashi and get her to reveal her source as he was aware that any interest he showed would only confirm her suspicions. So he decided to use a technique that he had recently mastered after observing his boss at close quarters.

He reached for his mobile phone inside his trouser pocket and pressed a key. A Bollywood item number began played loudly, indicating an incoming call. Fishing out the phone, Virkar smiled apologetically at Raashi, 'It's my boss,' he said, excusing himself.

'Yes sir...' he said into the phone.

Raashi broke into a sarcastic smile, 'Nice try, Inspector Virkar. Unfortunately, I've used this trick enough times to recognize it.'

Virkar ignored her and continued his conversation, 'Yes sir, I'll come right away.' He dumped all the papers lying on his desk into an open drawer, locked it with his free hand and put the key into his pocket. He rose from his chair, casting one last apologetic glance at the slightly taken-aback Raashi. Then he swiftly walked away, while continuing to speak into the phone. His colleagues around the room seemed amused though they managed to maintain a straight face.

Raashi's agitated voice called out to Virkar, 'I hope you know some better tricks, Inspector Virkar. Be ready with them the next time we meet.' But Virkar had already reached the exit door.

Raashi flung one final glance at Virkar's receding back. She then switched off the spy camera feature on the mobile phone she had placed on Virkar's table. *This one's not going to be easy*, she thought.

6

Moonlight bounced off the foam-capped waves of the Mumbai harbour as the Koli Queen, a small mechanized fishing trawler cut through the water, making its way out to sea. The two Koli fishermen, or nakhwas, were standing at the prow watching the water intently; their hands were itching to cast the blue nylon fishing trawl nets lying forlorn on the floor of the trawler. One of the nakhwas turned towards the single small cabin behind him and waved at the man at the wheel, pointing him towards the west. The man at the wheel waved back and turned the wheel towards what might be a potential cache of the few remaining shoals of fish near the Mumbai shoreline. Behind him, Virkar sat on a makeshift wooden bench on the open deck at the back of the trawler. It had been nailed to the wooden floor so as to keep it steady against the rise and fall of the boat. The trawler had set out around midnight and was scheduled to return to Mumbai only the next morning. Virkar reached out and opened a large thermocol icebox kept on one side of the wooden bench. He pried open the lid to reveal four bottles of Godfather Beer lying tantalizingly on a bed of crushed ice. Virkar popped open the cap of a chilled bottle and took a large swig directly from it. Letting the cold, malty fluid stream down his throat, he didn't make any attempt to suppress the small burp that conveyed his satisfaction. His free hand reached into a plastic bag lying next to him on the wooden bench and drew out a few greasy pieces of red hot Jhinga Koliwada enmeshed with raw onion curls. Popping the fried prawns and onion curls into his mouth, he let the succulent spices seep into his tongue and then began to masticate the fleshy treat. The juices triggered off his thought process and soon he was immersed in nostalgia.

Ever since he was a teenager, a midnight fishing trip was his escape from the big, bad world. The open deck of the boat was his refuge, the wooden bench his sanctum sanctorum. Something in the crests and troughs of the waves and the crispness of the midnight sea breeze always relaxed his wound-up senses, rejuvenating them to the sharpness he was known for. The beer and the prawns were just accompaniments to celebrate this happy state of mind.

Having grown up in Mumbai's Colaba Machhimar Nagar, a small Koli fishermen's community nestled between the residential skyscrapers of Cuffe Parade and the office towers of Nariman Point, Virkar was adept at deep-sea fishing. When he was young, he would accompany his father and his crew in the fishing trawlers that set out each morning in the hopes of filling their dol, or net, with a good catch. But with the change of times, the Koli fortunes dwindled and the community began encouraging their young to educate themselves in the Catholic schools nearby. As a result, Virkar got himself an English-medium education at the Holy Mary High School. He hit a small speed breaker when he didn't get into an engineering college and instead flirted with the idea of joining the Gotya Gang, a notorious group of chain snatchers and burglars. But, thankfully, good sense prevailed and he had gone to college, graduating with a degree in psychology and opting for the only job that would keep him out of trouble with the law—that of a policeman's. Indeed, he considered himself lucky when, today, most of the boys he had grown up with were either fishermen eking out a meagre living or wanted criminals living in constant fear of the bullet that would end their lives.

Virkar's thoughts now rolled with the sway of the boat. Sometime earlier that night, while examining the police artist's sketches of Nandu's likeness at his office, a massive pang of hunger hit Virkar and he realized that he had not eaten anything substantial in the past twenty-four hours. To top that, he suddenly remembered that he had been working non-stop for the past thirty-six hours. He decided that he had earned a break and quickly rushed to Pure Punjab Restaurant opposite the GPO to pick up a kilo of his favourite Jhinga Koliwada, a fried prawn delicacy. Many a visitor to Mumbai thought the Jhinga Koliwada was an authentic delicacy of Koli cuisine but, in fact, it was the Punjabi migrants from Pakistan settled among the small Koli community of Sion Koliwada who had concocted this unique and pungent preparation. Virkar couldn't care less. For him, Jhinga Koliwada was soul food. With the hot kilo of food secure in a plastic bag, Virkar quickly rode his Bullet to a brewery godown in Mazgaon and picked up half a dozen bottles of his favourite Godfather Beer from the friendly godown in-charge, who was always ready to indulge Virkar's fondness for this particular brand of beer that was so difficult to come by in Mumbai. Virkar had parked his Bullet in the shadows outside the godown and hailed a passing cab to his last stop for the night. The cab took him to Bhaucha Dhakka, otherwise known as the Ferry Wharf, where the Koli Queen was just getting ready to embark on its nightly fishing expedition. Two bottles of beer and two hundred-rupee notes bought him full occupancy of the wooden bench along with exclusive rights to the thermocol icebox.

◉

The moon now shone down on Virkar, its cool, white light illuminating the contours of every corner of the boat around him, while simultaneously creating patches of darkness that hid all the ugly, rough edges. The crests and troughs that the Koli Queen ploughed through provided the gentle, rocking sensation that served as a salve to Virkar's frayed nerves. Virkar took another swig of the amber beer—his second bottle—and tried to piece together the different strands of information he had been struggling to make sense of. He was, by now, quite sure that Nandu was no riffraff. He was a focused, intelligent and educated killer. Virkar was certain that Nandu was acting on his own, sans any accomplice as he had earlier believed. He set aside the empty bottle and watched the faraway city lights framing the shore. The light whirr of the boat's engine powering it through the water was the only sound in the still night. Virkar scratched the heavy stubble on his face. Only a person with a background in chemistry or engineering could have extracted ricin from castor. It required first-hand knowledge of castor beans and their toxicity as well as familiarity with the technical process of chromatography. Apart from being clever, Nandu also seemed to be a very good actor—he was able to pull off the role of a lowly daily-wage worker with apparent ease.

Virkar had found out that castor was grown in abundance in Andhra Pradesh, Gujarat, Orissa and Karnataka. The last bit of information was particularly interesting, since the vadapaowala had mentioned Nandu's Kannadiga origins. But what did a young man from Karnataka have against a police officer from Mumbai? Why Akurle?

Nandu's age indicated that he was probably just out of college, as did the fact that he was leaving his notes in old, metal compass boxes as a signature. Was there any significance in his use of the boxes? Or was it just a coincidence?

There was definitely no coincidence in his use of blood to write his notes. It indicated the strength of purpose in his obviously disturbed psyche. The blood had been analyzed and found to be human and of a common type, not providing much of a clue.

And then there was Dr Prabhat Bhandari. A search had thrown up four people with this name with the title 'doctor' living in Mumbai. Virkar had questioned all four but none had any knowledge of a young man from Karnataka harbouring a grudge against them. Virkar had wanted to put all four of them up at one place, in a hotel or a guest house, under his personal twenty-four-hour surveillance, but his boss had vetoed the idea. Instead, he had been instructed to put each of the four under standard police protection of a single police constable, but Virkar feared that it wouldn't be an adequate deterrent to the determined and devious Nandu. Besides, was Nandu his real name?

As the hours passed, the confusion in Virkar's mind only seemed to be rising as the bottles of beer and the Jhinga Koliwada finally started having an effect on his body. Lethargy crept into his muscles as the cool breeze lulled him into a sleepy haze. He picked up the icebox and kept it on the floor of the boat where he had earlier discarded the empty beer bottles and plastic bags. He stretched out on the bench, knowing that he had just a few hours before the Koli Queen turned around and deposited him back on shore. The last thought that popped into Virkar's mind was that Nandu's physical description and linguistic disposition combined with his superior scientific ability indicated that they were looking for a science or engineering graduate in Mumbai with his origins somewhere on the Maharashtra-Karnataka border. This profile narrowed the suspect list down to about a few hundred thousand young men. Virkar laughed out loud at his own predicament. *Naseeb gandu toh kya karega Pandu!* he thought as he surrendered to his fatigue and drifted off to sleep.

7

The killer opened the cheap, imitation leather briefcase that he was carrying and fished out a crisp visiting card. The neatly printed lettering on the visiting card didn't reveal his real name, but identified him as Sandesh Jejurikar (BPharm), Medical Representative, Kirti Pharmaceuticals. The killer handed it over to Police Constable Rane who had asked for it.

Rane, a sprightly man with thinning hair and shrewd, pea-sized eyes, had been instructed to closely monitor all visitors to one of the Dr Prabhat Bhandaris on Virkar's list. This particular doctor had a clinic at Framjee House, an old office building in the Dhobi Talao area of Mumbai. Rane had been handpicked by Virkar for this duty because he had, on many an occasion, displayed a keen sense of spotting potential troublemakers among mobs during riots. Like Virkar, Rane had been recently transferred to the Crime Branch from the Riot Control Police sub-unit, and was keen to prove his worth at his new job. He was diligently checking the identification of each and every visitor to Framjee House and had been especially strict with people who even remotely matched the police suspect Nandu's description.

Rane studied the slim, dark, bespectacled man standing in

front of him. He vaguely matched the police artist's sketch, but then so had many other young men who had walked in and out of the busy commercial building since early business hours.

Rane's suspicion radar was on as he scrutinized the visiting card in his hand. 'Please show me the identity card issued from your company as well,' he asked, keeping his tone casual. The killer opened his briefcase again and rummaged around in it. A small amount of nervousness had crept into his voice when he said, 'What's the matter, havaldar saheb? Why all this security?' Rane did not answer but waited patiently, watching the killer's face while he attempted to locate the ID card. The policeman tensed and slowly pulled himself to his full height, getting ready for action. But the killer simply pulled out a stiff laminated card dangling from a thin metal chain. 'Ah, here it is,' he said, holding it up in the air like a prize. Taking his time, he first shut his briefcase, placed it on the ground, stretched his limbs and yawned. By the time he handed his ID card to Rane, the policeman was at the end of his patience. Rane's sharp eyes quickly focused on the gawky, laminated picture of the annoying man in front of him, squinting at the ID number embossed on the card that bore the logo of Kirti Pharmaceuticals and a rubber-stamped company seal. It looked authentic enough.

Rane scratched his left ear; he was still not completely satisfied with it. He knew that this kind of a card could easily be generated at the thousands of Xerox/DTP/Lamination shops that dotted the city. Rane then said, 'Show me what's inside your briefcase.' The killer slowly lifted the case and opened it, turning it towards the Rane while making his reluctance evident. Rane paid him no mind and poked about in the briefcase. He found samples of medicines, company invoices, a boxed mobile phone and a steel tiffin, which, when opened, released a cloud of the rancid fumes of a long-devoured spicy meal.

Rane was still not happy. He now decided to use his secret weapon: a three-stage test that he had used on all the other men he had found suspicious. First, he called the receptionist at the clinic and asked her whether Dr Bhandari was expecting a medical representative (MR) from Kirti Pharmaceuticals. The receptionist confirmed that the doctor was indeed expecting an MR named Sandesh Jejurikar. Then Rane asked the killer to dial the boardline number of the offices of Kirti Pharmaceuticals. As soon as the number rang, Rane took the phone from the killer's hand and spoke to the receptionist, enquiring whether they had an employee called Sandesh Jejurikar. Satisfied at the positive response from the receptionist, Rane thanked her and handed the phone back to the killer. Rane smirked to himself and employed stage three of his test, his most devious move yet. 'Where is your native place, Jejurikar?' he asked in Marathi.

The killer looked a little taken aback by the suddenness of the question but replied in fluent Marathi, 'I'm from Jejuri, in Pune district.'

The constable raised a sly eyebrow. 'Jejuri? Isn't that where the samadhi of Sant Dnyaneshwar is?'

The killer answered in all earnestness. 'No, saheb, that is Alandi. Jejuri has the Khandoba Temple.'

Finally satisfied, Rane broke into a smile. 'Chalo, you can go on inside. The next time you are in your village temple, don't forget to say a little prayer for my wellbeing.'

The killer smiled back good-naturedly and nodded. 'Thank you, saheb. I will definitely try to remember.' He lifted his briefcase and headed up the wooden stairs to the clinic on the third floor.

As he walked up, the killer smiled to himself, happy in the knowledge that, once again, a policeman had been no match for him. He suppressed a laugh at how he had played mind games with Rane. He had deliberately stalled when asked to produce his ID card and he had also injected enough nervousness into his voice for it to get noticed. Nervousness was a common reaction of lay people when confronted by policemen; in fact, if he had not shown any sign of nervousness, the canny Rane would have picked this up as a suspicious sign. The killer wondered if he should have toyed with Rane a little longer, but then felt that it was for the better that he had not. He didn't have much time left for the task he had to perform now.

The killer reached his destination on the third floor and pushed open the opaque glass door in front of him on which the doctor's name was written in paint. As he walked into the small reception area of Dr Prabhat Bhandari's clinic, the receptionist, a wiry woman with henna-streaked hair, raised a quizzical eyebrow. 'Sandesh Jejurikar?' The killer nodded. The receptionist gave him an apologetic smile. 'Sorry, they are doing some kind of security exercise down there.' The killer just smiled back and shrugged.

The receptionist gestured towards a cabin. 'Dr Bhandari is free now.' The killer nodded his thanks, pushed open the cabin's door and entered.

Inside, a grey-haired man with a French beard that made him look a little like the IT revolutionary, Sam Pitroda, looked up from a sheet he was scrutinizing. He smiled at his visitor. 'Ah, you must be Jejurikar? So, what is this great promotional offer you told me about on the phone?'

8

The Bomb Detection and Disposal Squad of the Mumbai Police is a unique team of about 150 fearless men who continuously challenge death when they don their bomb suits, and with little else, go to work on something that can—literally—blow up in their faces. They do not have the safety of the sophisticated tools available to others in their profession around the world. In fact, theirs is a line of duty that depends on guts, keeping their wits intact...and sheer luck.

Today, while the bomb squad worked, the road across from Framjee House had been cleared and blocked and the entire area had been cordoned off for the fear of finding another explosive. Still, a pesky crowd of onlookers had gathered despite the police's attempts at shooing them away. In fact, they were debating whether to lathi charge the crowd to disperse them but they had been given strict orders to exercise restraint by the police commissioner himself, who had passed by the site while on the way to his office nearby.

Virkar had been standing impatiently at the edge of the police cordon for the past hour, waiting for the bomb squad to finish its search. Earlier, he had spent almost two hours getting a complete update from Constable Rane, who had somehow also managed to cross-question Dr Bhandari's hysterical receptionist. Virkar hadn't liked the picture that had emerged. The suspect, Nandu, who had changed his identity to kill Dr Bhandari, was now going by the name Sandesh Jejurikar and had, in fact, far cleverer and deadlier intentions than Virkar could have ever imagined. The receptionist said that Jejurikar, posing as a pharmaceutical company's sales representative, had entered Dr Bhandari's room on the pretext of discussing a lucrative offer of receiving a free high-end mobile phone on the placement of an order with Kirti Pharmaceuticals. The receptionist added, in a querulous voice, that she knew about this because the man's voice had been loud enough to be heard in the reception area.

Virkar had made a quick phone call to the CEO of Kirti Pharmaceuticals to confirm that such an offer had never existed. But there *was* an employee called Sandesh Jejurikar who had gone missing the day before. Virkar also found out that the physical description given by the CEO of his employee, Sandesh Jejurikar, didn't match that of the young man who had entered Framjee House.

Now, while being jostled by a couple of thousand curious onlookers and the plethora of TV news reporters, Virkar was praying that luck would be on their side and no live explosive device would be found in Dr Prabhat Bhandari's clinic.

As soon as he got the 'all-clear' signal from the chief of the bomb squad, Virkar rushed up to the third floor. He crossed his fingers, hoping against hope that he would not be welcomed with another cryptic message written in blood.

When he entered, the bomb squad officer gave him the thumbs up. 'I've checked the whole place twice,' he said. 'No live IED and no compass box...' He trailed off, noting the sudden discomfort on Virkar's face. He quickly stepped away, fearing that Virkar's stomach might react in response to the scenario in front of him—the effect of the single explosive device that had been used earlier in the day.

Dr Bhandari's headless body was slumped on the chair before Virkar. His head had been torn away from his body and its contents generously deposited across the wall behind in a large spattering of blood and gore. Tearing his eyes away from the trickling blood and gristle on the wall, Virkar turned his attention back to the headless body. Surprisingly, the rest of his body was intact except for his right hand which hung limply by his side and ended in a bleeding stump, his palm and fingers having been blown away from the wrist.

Virkar willed himself not to throw up but his insides knotted in revulsion and anger—anger, as he knew that this gruesome murder could have been prevented if only his bosses had implemented his idea for a joint protection detail for the doctors rather than just posting a constable at their doors.

He turned his attention back to the bomb squad officer who nodded towards the fragments of the mobile phone collected in a tray. Virkar bent down and examined them closely.

'Hmm…it looks like a small explosive was inserted into the phone which was detonated by a remote unit when Dr Bhandari started using it,' Virkar thought out aloud.

The bomb squad officer shook his head. 'It *was* the mobile phone that exploded, but I don't think that there was an explosive inserted *into* it. Otherwise we would have immediately seen traces of the explosive chemical on the body as well as on the fragments of the phone.' Virkar listened intently as the bomb squad officer continued. 'It's more likely that the suspect did something to the electronic circuitry and added a cheap duplicated battery rigged to explode by itself when the phone starts being used and heats up even a little. There have been cases where such a combination has led to extreme volatility.'

Virkar clicked his tongue in impatience. 'How soon can you give me a full report?' The bomb squad chief shrugged and pointed at the fragments. 'I don't know, saheb, since I don't have much of the mobile phone left to inspect.' Virkar threw him a frustrated look, and turned away to cast another glance at Dr Bhandari's body that was now being photographed and examined by the medical examiners and the forensic team. 'What I *can* tell you for sure is that the person who did this is an expert in technological matters and has a superb scientific brain,' added the bomb squad officer with grudging admiration.

'Hataa sawan ki ghataa, bhidu, kucch naya bataa,' muttered Virkar to himself.

Suddenly, the sharp ringing of a mobile phone cut through the air of the now crowded room. Everyone froze. They looked at each other and then around them, half-expecting to find an unexploded mobile phone lying undetected somewhere. Virkar sheepishly pulled out the ringing phone from his pocket and held it up for all to see. The policemen went back to their respective work, tittering with embarrassment. Virkar's phone flashed the Crime Branch headquarters' number on its screen. Speaking loudly enough for everyone to hear, he remarked, 'Apun log toh hain ghanti ke ghulam.' Everyone in the room laughed out loud.

Virkar smiled and waved his hands to quieten the men as he took the call.

'Hello?' he said.

An on-duty sub-inspector gushed breathlessly into the phone. 'Vir-Virkar saheb, a man calling himself Sandesh Jejurikar has just walked into the Tank Bunder Police Station with a compass box.'

9

Raashi and her cameraman were standing in front of the young, dazed-looking man who had identified himself as Sandesh Jejurikar and who looked as though he had spent a day rolling around in a grass patch. Raashi's mike was hovering near his face in an attempt to catch any sort of coherent sound bite. 'How did you get the compass box?' she asked the young man for the umpteenth time. She had been quite patient until now, but was slowly realizing that she may not get anything out of the man who still seemed to be under the influence of some drug. Raashi also kept an eye on the entrance of the Tank Bunder Police Station, half-expecting to see the swarthy Inspector Virkar come tearing through it and putting an end to the exposé she had managed to bribe her way into. She had offered a reward to any informer who would let her know anything about the case that had been kept tightly under wraps so far.

Raashi's desperate attempt had paid off and a quick call had brought her running to the police station, baying for her Breaking News. 'Please…tell me something…anything…about yourself.' The desperation that could now be heard in her voice surprisingly had its effect. The young man began to speak in a halting voice. He talked about his childhood—growing up in the temple town of Jejuri in the Pune district; how he had studied hard and prayed to Khandoba every day to get him into University of Pune's BPharm course; how he had come to Mumbai and got his first job at Kirti Pharmaceuticals; how he was the star performer in his department, etcetera.

Raashi gritted her teeth with impatience. She wanted to cut short the babbling barrage of useless information but decided to let him get warmed up before steering him towards what she really wanted to know. Suddenly, a familiar booming voice cut through the young man's prattle. 'What's going on?'

Before Raashi could react, Sandesh was pulled away into the interrogation room by the two flustered-looking constables who had earlier generously given her the access she had desired. No stranger to quickly changing scenarios, the sharp-witted Raashi immediately turned her mike and cameraman towards Inspector Virkar. She didn't want to lose this opportunity to grill the man who had brushed her off at their last meeting.

'Inspector Virkar, another compass box has been found and the man who has brought it in has no idea where he got it from. What do you have to say about this?'

Virkar's voice cut through Raashi's shrill pitch. 'Have you seen the compass box?' he asked, shooting her a pointed look.

Raashi stuttered a quick, 'No.'

'Then how can you be sure that such a compass box exists?' asked Virkar dismissively.

'I have been informed by reliable sources,' Raashi shot back.

'Acchha...so tell me, who are your sources, madam? Let me also see how reliable they are.'

Raashi flushed. 'I cannot reveal my sources.'

Virkar cocked an eyebrow at her and smiled. 'That's very thoughtful of you. You have saved them from losing their jobs.

Now if you will excuse me, I have to do mine.'

Raashi knew that she was checkmated, but flung a last barb at the departing Virkar. 'We'll see how good you are at yours. We are watching and waiting…and so is the public.' Virkar let that one bounce off his back as he strode into the interrogation room. Raashi turned to the camera. 'That was Inspector Virkar, who is rumoured to be responsible for the many slip-ups that have made this case more difficult than it really is. We shall be talking to his superiors at the Crime Branch to seek absolute clarity on the issue. With camera person Raju Bhonsale, this is Raashi Hunerwal for *Crime Update*.'

Inside the interrogation room, the young man—who had now gained a semblance of coherence—was telling Virkar about the sequence of events that had brought him to the Tank Bunder Police Station. His last memory of the previous night was of stopping for a quick drink at the Gokul Bar behind The Taj Mahal Hotel where he had bumped into a slim, young man called Nandu in the crowded urinal, and how the well-spoken and intelligent Nandu had later befriended him at the corner table in the air-conditioned section frequented by medical representatives. Nandu had then ordered half a bottle of Old Monk, and after a few drinks and a lot of talking, had got him totally drunk. The young man couldn't remember anything after that. He had recovered from his drugged state sometime earlier this evening to find himself in the small jungle-like area in front of the Hindustan Lever Mill in Sewree.

Virkar let out an audible sigh. So that was how the killer got hold of Sandesh Jejurikar's Kirti Pharmaceutical employee card.

'I don't know anything about the compass box, Inspector saheb,' continued Sandesh, now close to tears. 'It was only when I had slightly recovered from my daze that I noticed it stuffed into my trouser pocket. It was wrapped in brown paper with a message written on it.' Virkar picked up the brown paper packet lying on the table next to the compass box. The small, neat block letters written on it said: GO TO THE NEAREST POLICE STATION.

Sandesh's pleading eyes met Virkar's. 'I came here, saheb. It took a little time as I had to walk and keep asking people for directions,' he said. Virkar now turned his attention to the compass box on the table. On opening it, he found another note written in blood. This one plainly said: Find Nigel Colasco.

This time, the name seemed vaguely familiar, but before Virkar could jog his memory, the on-duty sub-Inspector who was hovering nearby, spoke up. 'Virkar saheb, Nigel Colasco is a lawyer and popular NGO activist who is well connected with the Mumbai police.'

Virkar turned towards him. 'Where is he based?' The sub-inspector, desperate to involve himself in the high-profile case, said eagerly, 'His NGO office is situated on P. D'Mello Road near the Cotton Green station.' As Virkar got up to go, the sub-inspector cleared his throat. He clearly did not want to miss his chance of ingratiating himself to an officer from the Crime Branch. 'Inspector saheb, if you're leaving to find Colasco, you don't have to go far. He's sitting with our senior inspector in his cabin,' the man said in a meaningful tone. 'Our senior inspector saw the note and immediately summoned him, long before you arrived.' Virkar stopped in his tracks, realizing to his dismay that he was going to have to get involved in departmental and jurisdictional politics. The sub-inspector lowered his voice till it was barely audible. 'Saheb, our senior inspector is a very… er…ambitious man.' Virkar hated these opportunistic officers who tried to muscle their way into investigations in the hope of gaining some credit.

Virkar sighed. 'Na jaal, na jhinga, pun dariya mein khas-khas.'

10

The forty-two-inch flatscreen television in ACP Wagh's living room now came alive with the 9.00 p.m. news playing on the CrimeNews channel. ACP Wagh had had a rough day at the Crime Branch and had just poured himself his first peg of Old Monk. He had received an SMS from Raashi earlier in the day, requesting him to tune into *Crime Update* that evening. The overly made-up reporter appeared on the screen, the sky-blue contact lenses in her eyes flickering with determination as she stood outside Framjee House, a crowd of onlookers and policemen in the backdrop. She began by bringing viewers up-to-date with the gruesome murder of Dr Prabhat Bhandari and then continued, 'Today, in Breaking News brought to you exclusively by *Crime Update*, we reveal the story behind the cover-up of a deadly serial killer.' Wagh took a large swig of his Old Monk, riveted by the young woman's dramatic delivery. 'This heinous criminal is now known in police circles as the Compass Box Killer. Reliable sources have informed us that this serial killer leaves behind a student's geometry box next to the body of his victim. Each compass box has a note written in blood, supposedly his own, telling us the name of his next victim.' Raashi paused and smirked at the camera. 'What are the police doing about this killer's deadly rampage? We questioned the officer in charge of the investigation, Inspector Virkar, but he had only this to say…' The image on the screen now cut to a sour-looking Virkar, who intoned, 'Who are your sources?' This was played in a loop with Virkar repeating, 'Who are your sources?' ad nauseum.

When all the comic potential of Virkar's pithy line had been extracted to the hilt, Raashi came back on the screen, looking visibly bewildered.

'Good acting, lady,' Wagh smirked, draining the last of his Old Monk.

Raashi raised a quizzical eyebrow, slowly milking the moment. 'We would like to advise Inspector Virkar that instead of asking such questions from us, he should concentrate on his investigation which is fast spinning out of control. The Compass Box Killer has already struck twice. We have learnt from reliable sources that he has delivered yet another compass box naming his next victim. Senior police officers remain unavailable for comment and we dare not ask Inspector Virkar for more information because all he will say is…' The scene once again cut to Virkar mouthing, 'Who are your sources? Who are your sources? Who are your sources?'

Raashi appeared on the screen once again, her voice now rising theatrically and her index finger jabbing the air. 'The people want *answers* to these killings. We want to know *who* the next victim on the list is so we can put him under surveillance. The unfortunate episode of Dr Prabhat Bhandari's death should *not* be repeated.' Raashi took a deep breath and continued, 'We, the people of Mumbai, are *not* afraid. But will the police listen to us—the citizens, the common man? Or will another person be sacrificed like Dr Bhandari?'

Raashi walked with the mike, unfazed by the thronging crowd collecting behind her. 'Will the police take any action against

Inspector Virkar for not being able to save the life of an honest, innocent doctor, despite having received a warning that he is the next victim?' Raashi finished with the triumphant flourish of a rabble-rouser who has achieved her objective.

ACP Wagh reached for the remote and switched the television off. He had seen enough. He glanced at the three mobile phones neatly laid out on the white hand towel on the small glass side table next to the sofa he was sitting on. He picked them up one by one and turned them off. He sank back into his plush leather sofa, recalling Virkar's plea to save Dr Bhandari by requesting he oversee the twenty-four-hour protection detail for all the potential victims. ACP Wagh shrugged off his guilt and coldly evaluated the facts. Self-preservation was his natural instinct and he had honed it to perfection over the years. He began formulating his course of action which, basically, involved doing nothing. He knew that the media would soon start hounding him. He was, after all, Virkar's boss, the venerated ACP of the Crime Branch's murder squad. Wagh steepled his fingers, an idea forming in his mind. He decided to remain unavailable for media comments and let the vultures make Virkar their scapegoat. Only when the media went hoarse blaming Virkar for the second killing by being lax about following the clues would he step in and make a sweeping statement that would appease the media hounds and smoothen out the ruffled feathers of his own superiors. He made a mental note to spend some time with this upstart Virkar someday and teach him a thing or two about being media-savvy—that is, if the poor fellow survived this case.

Having neatly worked out the plot in his head, ACP Wagh smiled to himself and glanced at his wristwatch, wondering whether he had enough time to catch the night show of any movie. It would have started by now, which suited him perfectly.

Years of experience had taught him that night shows were the best possible excuse for not being available when all hell was breaking loose elsewhere in the city. After all, no one could begrudge a busy police officer his recreation time, his escape from the harshness of his daily grind. He quickly rose to his feet and called out an offer to his wife who was cooking in the kitchen—an offer he knew she wouldn't refuse. 'Lila, let's go and watch the latest Aamir Khan film.'

11

Virkar rode his Bullet down the dark, empty streets of early-morning Mumbai. Under normal circumstances, Virkar always wore his helmet, but today he wanted to feel the cool air whip his hair at the roots. The heat generated in his system over the past few hours had bothered him enough to hop on to his Bullet for his occasional 'dimaag ka dahi' early-morning rides. He found these to be extremely therapeutic.

For the past few hours, the image of him foolishly repeating, 'Who are your sources?' had worn his patience to the bone. 'Hunterwali' had lived up to her name. To add fuel to the fire, the repressed mirth in the eyes of all the night-duty policemen at his office had ignited his already simmering temper. A sympathetic comment by an old constable had made him lash out at him, spewing vitriol on the poor soul. By the time Virkar managed to control himself, the mirth in everyone's eyes had changed to sympathy. Virkar decided that he had better do something quickly, lest he lose everyone's respect too. He had left his office in a huff, aching for the comfort offered by a bottle of Godfather but deciding that the situation called for more drastic action.

Virkar's Bullet sped towards the address he had extracted

from the scared mobile phone company executive (being in the police had its uses). The object of his anger, Raashi Hunerwal, aka 'Hunterwali', apparently had a flat in a cooperative housing society in Andheri West. In Virkar's fuming mind, the only way he could seek retribution was by having it out, fair and square, with the perpetrator of the injustice that had been heaped on him. He was going to have a firm chat with her, knock some much-needed sense in that pouty, pretty head of hers and show her what her flippant and foolish insinuations could do to his career. In his mind, Virkar started building scenarios that all ended with Raashi falling at his feet and apologizing profusely, having been shown the error of her ways. Virkar could already taste the triumph of putting her in her place.

But as the wind swept over the contours of his hardened face, he began to calm down; gradually, the waves of self-righteous anger began to retract from his mind. He slowed down the Bullet, abandoning his 'Mission Hunterwali'. It never paid to unleash your wrath on the female species, especially not on a pesky crime reporter. Nevertheless, Virkar still felt the sharp sting of having been the object of ridicule that had played out on television for all to watch. Raashi's sly insinuation that he had been lax about his work and was indirectly responsible for Dr Bhandari's death had hurt him to the very core. Virkar had always been known to stick to his guns as an officer and was considered honest and upright to a fault. He was used to investigating his cases with utmost sincerity, delivering the desired results and quickly moving on to the next case without resting on past laurels. And now Raashi had cast aspersions on his abilities.

Being hounded by media was new to Virkar and he grudgingly admitted to himself that he was out of his depth in this crisis. In the ten years he had been posted in Gadchiroli fighting Maoists, he had never encountered such backlash for not having shared information with the press. In fact, he was used to withholding information with full cooperation from the media so that the suspects didn't know the police's next move and could be caught unawares. Virkar suddenly wished he were back in the jungles of Gadchiroli under the moonlit sky with nothing but a bullet to separate him from his enemy. At least then he could see and feel the danger as it came for him.

As he cruised along the empty Worli sea face, he glanced at the turn for the Bandra-Worli Sea Link, itching to turn the Bullet and drive down it full throttle. But he kept himself in check, reminding himself that he was an officer of the law and couldn't afford to break rules. He suddenly wondered what had caused a young, intelligent man like Nandu to become a hardcore criminal. He thought of the few times he had flirted with the idea of indulging in petty crime in his youth and sighed with relief at having never crossed that dangerous line.

Virkar gunned the Bullet back into action; the soaring phut-phut-phut of the bike was music to his ears as he rode towards Prabhadevi onto Mahim Causeway and turned off to the Western Express Highway to the right. At that time of the morning, he cleared the twenty-four kilometre distance to the Dahisar check naka in fifteen minutes flat. Riding headlong against the wind invigorated Virkar's troubled senses and he was ready for the refreshing jolt of the early-morning 'Nescoffee' sold at the small shacks by the check naka.

There, sitting amongst flatulent truck drivers and half-asleep transporters from every corner of India, Virkar finally felt the belligerence inside him melt away. As he let the final drop of the strong, sweet, dirt-brown liquid trickle down his throat, Virkar was ready to face the media backlash that the first rays of the sun would bring, wrapped in fresh newspapers.

12

Nigel Colasco had stepped out of his house after five days, but even after an hour on the streets, he was getting increasingly restless because of the constant police presence around him. However, he was still greeting everyone he met with his customary smile that stretched across a face that had been weathered by years of exposure to the sun. After all, he was a supremely genial man who had acquired the enviable reputation of being known as a patient and intrepid crusader for the rights of slum children.

Having grown up in a devout East-Indian Catholic family in Bandra, Colasco had developed a passion for charitable work at an early age. Under the tutelage of the priests of his parish, he had spent years in slums and nearby villages, giving hours and hours of his time and resources to every lost cause. As an adult, he had come into his own and established his NGO while continuing to dedicate his every waking hour to the upliftment of the deprived and weaker sections of society. But for the past five days, he and all his actions had become the subject of intense scrutiny and speculation in the media. Why was Nigel Colasco the Compass Box Killer's next victim? Nosy, self-propelled media 'investigators' had sifted through each little sinew of his body of work in the courts and slums of Mumbai. Overzealous TV anchors were thrusting their mikes towards any mouth that was willing to let its tongue wag. Even the watchmen, car cleaners, dhobis and maids from Colasco's neighbourhood near Mount Mary Steps in Bandra were not spared in the hope of any grain of 'exclusive' information that they might unearth about him. Unfortunately for the media, Colasco's clean life and straightforward dealings did nothing to help spin the rumour mill that could feed the media frenzy. To the great disappointment of channel crusaders, Colasco, now in his mid-forties, had had a perfectly strait-laced career that had begun with an assistantship at a small labour law practice firm and thereafter moved towards him taking up the cudgels for the downtrodden as an extension of his charitable work. They had come flocking to him as he began spending his free hours by working in the myriad slums of Mumbai. Soon, what was an avocation had become a full-time vocation as Nigel opened the NGO, Slum Baalak Suraksha. The plaudits that his stellar work earned in helping slum children get educated and find employment had led to Nigel becoming a familiar face at government offices. The somnolent officials were only too happy to help someone who was doing their job for them. Awards and accolades swiftly began to adorn the cabinets in the reception area of his office while his simple home in Bandra became a pit stop for every visiting foreign dignitary who felt it was their moral duty to empathize with the wretched and poor in India.

After his name was discovered written in blood on a piece of paper, he had been questioned and re-questioned by the police for two straight days, first at the Tank Bunder Police Station, then at the Crime Branch headquarters and finally in the comfort of his small, two-bedroom, sparsely-furnished apartment in Julia Dream Cooperative Housing Society. After ensuring that he had a clean record and knew nothing of the killer's motive, the police brass had placed him under twenty-four-hour police protection. To escape the shrill-voiced reporters clamouring outside his apartment building thirsting to know how he was feeling, Colasco had decided to stay home until their interest in him died down. Whenever he wanted to step out of his house, he was escorted by a battery of policemen otherwise lined up outside his door. By the fifth day, though, he had had enough of the self-confinement and the crowd of reporters had thinned.

Colasco had been itching to venture out ever since the police investigation had started, not because he was anxious to step into danger, but because he felt that his absence from the slums would be construed as a sign of fear by the slum children who idolized him.

After spending an hour with the children, Colasco went back to his flat, flanked on both sides by a small police contingent led by the now infamous Inspector Virkar, the person who had become the media's 'whipping boy' over the past five days. As he walked braving the mid-morning sun, Colasco read the agony written on Virkar's face. Like him, Virkar, too, had become the city's favourite topic of dinner-table conversations.

Virkar wiped the sweat from his brow. It was an unbearably hot day and the sun beat down relentlessly from the clear sky. He had earlier been summoned to the Crime Branch headquarters to be severely reprimanded for his slip-up with the media and had been forbidden from making any more statements to the press. In fact, he had specifically been advised to avoid all eye contact with the bite-hungry mike-wielders. And though several people had called for Virkar's resignation, transfer, or at least to have him taken off the case, he had been retained by his seniors.

ACP Wagh had taken Virkar aside and told him not to take things personally. Virkar could have sworn that he saw a small smile playing on Wagh's fat lips. Though Virkar had simply nodded in obeisance to his boss's advice, he had actually taken things to heart. Ignoring the barbs flying in all directions, he had sprung into action, determined to not be made a fool of again anytime soon. He had created a squad of crack policemen chosen from various sub-units and had instituted a three-shift, twenty-four-hour supervision module for Nigel Colasco which left no room for any lapses. He had cordoned off Julia Dream Society and furnished every resident with special photo ID cards that were checked every time they came in or went out of the building premises. A far better composite sketch of the suspect, Nandu, aka the Compass Box Killer, had been made with the help of the real Sandesh. This sketch was circulated in the Julia Dream Society and sent to every police station and government office, both small and large. Policemen personally paid a visit to the local political party workers in the slums and chawls under their jurisdiction and asked them to keep a lookout for suspicious people who resembled the police sketch.

A massive naka bandi or road check exercise was launched across Mumbai. Some plainclothes policemen masquerading as Brihan Mumbai Municipal Corporation workers were stationed across the road from Julia Dream Society, pretending to dig up the road. Virkar had gone as far as to depute two women police constables to dress up as kelewalis who roamed the neighbourhood with tokris laden with bananas, selling them to anyone who looked suspicious. This did get a few sneers from their male colleagues in the Crime Branch, but after two days, this move began to draw grudging admiration from the same men as they wised up to the advantages of an unsuspecting target being accosted by someone as innocuous as a banana seller in a traditional Marathi nine-yard saree.

However hard he tried, though, Virkar was not able to shake off the ever-looming presence of his bête noire, Raashi 'Hunterwali', who had positioned herself in the media cordon and doggedly monitored Colasco's every movement. To Virkar, it felt like she was monitoring *him* and not Colasco. Regardless of where Virkar stood on the Society's compound, he could feel Raashi's sky-blue contact lenses boring a hole in the back of his head. He tried to shake off the feeling and changed his position frequently. But whenever he stole a glance at her from the corner of his eyes, he caught her looking directly at him. Virkar was at his wit's end trying to concentrate on the task at hand and Raashi's constant presence was a distraction he didn't appreciate. In the midst of all that was going on, Virkar would take some time out and escape to a quiet corner on the building's terrace where he would turn his face heavenwards and plead for some relief from Hunterwali's nauseating scrutiny.

By the fifth day of the vigil outside Colasco's home, the policemen posted on the security detail began to relax a little, gathering in small groups for frequent chitchats and chai. Noticing their lax attitude, Virkar decided to wind them up again. He called for a quick emergency meeting and told them that he had been informed that the Hunterwali's cameraman had shot a few of them napping on his camera and that she had sent the CD to the Crime Branch headquarters. Virkar casually let slip that he didn't know who was on the CD but was expecting a call at any moment from his bosses. The policemen shuffled their feet, exchanging sheepish looks. Within minutes, each of them had resumed his duty, doubly alert and hoping against hope that *they* weren't the ones on the CD.

As he surveyed the policemen's tense faces, Virkar couldn't help feeling a little ashamed about his little deception. However, he felt better when saw their sharp expressions, once again on the alert for the person who had made a bloody declaration to kill the man they were here to protect.

13

'I've been working as a technician for the past four years at my uncle's electronic repair shop in Malad,' said the killer. His oily, slicked-back hair and the soorma in his eyes were in contrast with his frayed jeans and red T-shirt that read 'Reabockk' on the front. Barkat Ali was unimpressed. For one, he was used to such tall claims being made to him. Everyone who wanted a job at the three-decade-old Barkat Alitronics, his electrical repair and maintenance shop in Dharavi, claimed that he was God's gift to 'electricianity'. He laughed at the word he had coined. Most of these braggarts didn't know how to connect two wires to save their lives. And this scrawny, young scrap of a boy who looked like he was still waiting for puberty to hit, seemed to be even less proficient at what Barkat Ali considered a dying art. He spat out copious amounts of pan-stained saliva and wiped his mouth with his calloused fingers. The killer stared at the healed burn marks on Barkat Ali's fingers. Noticing the young candidate's keen interest in his lacerated fingers, Barkat Ali offered an explanation. 'Thirty years of receiving electrical shocks,' he said, menacingly dangling his fingers literally under the killer's nose.

The killer didn't flinch; instead he retorted with, 'I can't compete with that. I've just worked four years *without* receiving any electrical shocks.'

Barkat Ali raised a sneering eyebrow. The killer's spunky response had touched a raw nerve. 'Dedh shaane, have you come to ask for a job or to show me how smart you are, eh?'

The killer stared back, undeterred. 'How does it matter? You've already decided not to give me the job, without even testing my skills and seeing if I'm good enough.'

Barkat Ali narrowed his eyes. He was a busy man and was used to taking spot decisions, but this young upstart had dared to challenge his experience. He was not going to let it pass without humiliating this langoor. 'Come, let's find out how good you are,' Barkat Ali barked. Without another word, he turned and walked into the deep, dark portals of his shack-like shop. The killer followed him silently. Barkat Ali led him through a narrow corridor lined with wooden shelves laden with electrical spare parts of every type and size. What the killer had initially thought to be a small shop turned out to be just the front of a large godown into which Barkat Ali now ushered him. Inside the cavernous space, workmen slaved over tables lined all the way to the tin walls on all four sides. The killer swept his eyes across the godown, taking in the all the toasters, microwaves, washing machines, electrical irons and other household appliances strewn about in various stages of repair. Barkat Ali's smug voice turned the killer's attention back towards him. 'Toh, mere shock-proof bhidu, ready for your entrance test?'

The killer nodded, not knowing what was in store but suspecting that it was something that would pose a big challenge to him. Barkat Ali pointed at an old black-and-white television set lying on a dusty table next to him. As he reached out and patted it fondly, fine grains of dust rose from the cheap laminate top. 'My first TV,' said Barkat Ali, pride oozing from his voice. The killer looked at the ancient television set; a dull grey convex screen stared blankly back at him. The brand name, EC TV, was emblazoned on one side of the television set just above a bunch of chunky chrome knobs. Barkat Ali's voice cut through the dank air of the godown. 'Black and white. Valve technology. Specially made by the Government of India as the "People's TV". This particular set has not worked for more years than I can count.'

The killer continued to stare at the television set that had obviously seen better days, wondering if the circuit board was still inside it.

'Toh, mere Bijli kay PhD, what are you waiting for? Make it work...go on!' Barkat Ali chuckled. The killer lifted a screwdriver lying on the table, walked around the television and began to unscrew the wooden back cover of the TV set. Barkat Ali stood watching him for a few moments, inviting the other workmen to join him by chuckling loudly. By the time the killer had unscrewed the back off, Barkat Ali had lost interest and walked back to the shop front. 'Shaana kauwa!' he had guffawed, throwing the boy a pitiful look.

The killer rolled up his jeans and sat down on the dusty floor to work. He turned his attention to the insides of the ancient TV. This would require his complete concentration. He realized that he would need a soldering iron as he applied pressure and extricated the detachable circuit board. The killer smiled to himself as his sharp eyes surveyed the jumble of the small resistors welded across the board. He had fixed many such circuits a long time ago, and unlike what he had thought earlier, this was not going to pose too much of a challenge to him. Suppressing his laughter, the killer glanced up at the figure of Barkat Ali disappearing down the corridor. 'Thirty years of practical experience is no match for five years of quality education,' he muttered under his breath. He was going to get this dinosaur of a TV to work, and he was going to get the job at Barkat Alitronics, even if he had to put up with Barkat Ali's stupid, insulting habit of name-calling. The next phase of his plan depended entirely on the success of this challenge and there was no way that he would turn back now.

14

The police party passed an open garbage dump. The previous night's drizzle had wet the refuse through and through. Now in the baking sun, the stench was rising and spreading, threatening to choke the life out of the toughest nostrils. Virkar's attention was drawn to the scurrying movements around the garbage dump. His sharp gaze focused on what looked like mongrel pups, but as his eyes zeroed in on one of the wallowing black creatures, he realized that they were not pups but rats! Giant black rats, gorging on the feast of Mumbai's leftovers. Virkar turned his attention back to the slippery, slushy path that he and about twenty of his best policemen were trying to navigate on their way to a function to felicitate the man they were all escorting: Nigel Colasco. Despite several warnings, Colasco had insisted on attending this particular event. It was inside the dirtiest, least-developed part of Dharavi called Kunjupada that sat on the lip of the swampy nullah disguised as the Mithi River. Colasco's sentimental attachment to this event went back almost twenty years to when he had held his first workshop for slum children at that very place. The people from the hutments that lay on that dark, damp patch revered Colasco. Every year, on the auspicious occasion of the Phitrabhoomi Devi festival, the Kunjupada Hutment Committee gave special prizes that were personally handed out by Colasco to the children of the slum. Despite the looming death threat over him, Colasco had insisted on making the trip to Kunjupada. Virkar had relented only after having personally surveyed the site with his men and rounding up all known troublemakers from the area as a cautionary measure. The residents of Kunjupada were miffed at the police presence, especially since they believed that this was perhaps the safest place for their hero, Colasco. Almost all their lives had been touched by Colasco's benevolence in one way or another, so why would any one of them kill their benefactor?

Having safely waded through the small crowd of impatient-looking parents and slum children gathered for the felicitation, the police party approached the makeshift wooden dais set up on one side of the small, open maidan between the tin huts. Virkar quickly positioned his entire contingent in strategic places around the wooden dais and only then gave the nod to the organizers of the function to begin the proceedings.

A group of local Kunjupada elders stepped forward with garlands and sweets led by a thin, white-haired, kurta-lungi-clad man, who had the pompous bearing of a small-time politician. Virkar stepped forward and stopped the advancing group; he checked every garland personally, ruffling the flowers with a metal detector in search of any concealed weapons. 'Aren't you taking things too far, Inspector saheb?' asked the lungi-clad man. Virkar continued with his inspection without acknowledging the man's presence or question. 'You are making us feel as though we are terrorists and Colasco saheb is the Prime Minister,' the lungi-clad man continued in a cantankerous tone. Virkar ignored him once again.

'I'm speaking to you, Inspector. Do you know who I am?'

the man's voice had now risen above the din of the clamouring slum children.

This time Virkar turned towards him. 'I know who you are, Mr Ramaswami Putharan. You've been the Municipal Corporator for this area twice during the eighties. However, my information tells me that you lost your deposit in the last election.' Putharan looked like he had been slapped. Making apoplectic noises, he tried to come up with an appropriate answer but couldn't find the words.

Suddenly, Virkar's eyes fell on a silver thali laden with what looked like malai pedas. 'What's this?' he enquired.

The wizened, shrunken old lady who stood teetering under the weight of the silver thali was not used to being directly addressed by policemen. She nervously shifted her weight from one foot to another, tongue-tied. 'It's Phitrabhoomi Devi maa's prasad,' interjected Putharan, having finally found his tongue.

'Sorry, I can't allow this,' said Virkar sternly.

The old lady timidly spoke up. 'But, beta, this is the Devi maa's prasad. I've brought it from the mandir myself.'

Virkar signalled one of his men to take the thali from her hands. 'Sorry, maaji, no prasad for Mr Colasco.'

A policeman tried to take the thali from the old woman who looked close to tears. Suddenly, Putharan stepped forward and took the thali from her before the policeman could do so.

He glared at Virkar. 'Are you saying that you're not going to allow us to practice our rituals?'

It was Virkar's turn to be tongue-tied. He knew that Putharan had seized the one weakness in the policing system of India—the fear of hurting religious sentiments. Anything that Virkar said or did now could be blown out of proportion, and the situation could easily turn nasty. *Attack is the best form of defence*, he thought, and said calmly, 'Mr Colasco's life is under threat. The prasad could be poisoned.'

But Putharan was not going to give up so easily. He raised the thali above his head theatrically, and, speaking loud enough to be heard by everyone gathered in the small ground, said, 'Are you saying that Devi maa's prasad has been purposely poisoned by us?'

A rumble of discontent rippled through the crowd. Virkar was aware of the failed politician's attempts to squeeze sympathy for himself out of every opportunity. But he was not going to allow it. 'Well, if it is not poisoned, please have some before offering it to Mr Colasco,' he suggested. Putharan's face suddenly deflated like a balloon. 'I...er...it's my fast today,' he finally managed.

He's good. No wonder he is a politician. Virkar turned to the old lady. 'Then maybe maaji can have some before offering it to Mr Colasco?'

The old lady shrunk a few more inches. 'I'm also fasting. I've been fasting for the past sixty years. I mean...every year on this day.'

Virkar knew that he had the advantage. He turned to the gathered crowd and said, 'I fear that this prasad may be poisoned. Is there anyone here who would like to taste the prasad before offering it to Mr Colasco?' The group of people stared at the ground in silence. No one raised a hand or made eye contact.

Suddenly, out of the corner of his eye, Virkar noticed that Raashi and her cameraman were standing on one side of the stage. The reporter, as always, was power-dressed, looking totally incongruous in their current setting. Virkar was about to curse under his breath, as was his usual practice whenever he saw her, but stopped when he noticed the admiring look on her face. Virkar was confused. He was expecting a fresh round of fighting but her expression seemed to indicate otherwise.

'Inspector Virkar, can we please start the function?' Colasco's clipped words cut through Virkar's thoughts. He and the policeman with the thali stepped away from the group and everyone quickly took their positions on the dais. As was the usual practice over the years, Colasco stepped up to the podium, ready to start announcing the prize winners. But as soon as he held the mike, a small flame burst out from the top of his head, and he fell on to the wooden dais, shaking uncontrollably while trying to wrench himself away from the steel mike that was stuck to the burning skin of his palms.

15

W*ood is a bad conductor of electricity—that's why he's still alive.* The realization flashed through Virkar's mind as he watched Colasco writhing on the wooden dais. If it hadn't been for the wood, Colasco would have died instantaneously, given that the shock had been potent enough to cause a flame to emanate from his body.

However, the electrically-charged steel mike stand burning Colasco's palms was the biggest deterrent to providing him with any sort of aid. If Virkar touched either the mike or Colasco, he, too, would get a severe shock. There was no question of pulling them apart with his hands. His eyes darted over the dais looking for something he could use to pry them apart, even as utter chaos broke out among the audience. Around him, the frightened slum elders started withdrawing from the scene, afraid that the flames would leap out at them and spread everywhere. Women were grabbing their screaming children and beating a hasty exit. Virkar's police contingent, too, was rooted to its spot, not knowing how to react in this moment of crisis.

Suddenly, Virkar saw a discarded cardboard placard lying on the dusty floor. A handwritten message on it read: 'East or West,

Nigel Colasco is the Best'. But what had actually caught Virkar's attention was the wooden stake that had held the sign up earlier. In one smooth motion, he scooped up the placard and ripped away the wooden stake. Hopping on to the dais, he took a stab at the steel mike with the stake, flinching as he saw Colasco's palm gradually starting to char. Virkar realized that, to break the flow of the electric current, he needed to wedge the stake between Colasco's hand and the mike. Taking care not to touch the electrified steel, Virkar leaned closer, his keen eyes searched for an opening between Colasco's fingers. He prodded Colasco's hand, feeling his vice-like grip on the steel mike stand. Noticing a small gap in the space between Colasco's right forefinger and thumb, he tried to drive the sharp end of the stake through it. But the gap was not big enough for the wooden stake to penetrate deep enough to dislodge the charged mike stand.

By now, Colasco had started frothing at the mouth, muttering incoherently. Virkar threw the stake aside; there was no time for niceties. The only way he could get the steel mike away from Colasco was if Colasco himself opened his tightly-clenched fingers. Without further thought, Virkar stomped on Colasco's chest with all his might. The base of his leather police boot connected with Colasco's heart with a massive 'thump'. Virkar felt pinpricks of current running up his leg—he knew the electricity had entered his boot through the tiny metal nails embedded in the sole of his service boots. Colasco's system registered a severe shock, making him cough out loud. Suddenly, his body stopped shivering, his palm flew open and his fingers let go of the steel mike which then rolled off the stage and on to the ground. An eager young police constable jumped on to the dais to help lift Colasco off the floor, but before he could touch him, Virkar barked, 'Thamb! Electricity could still be running through his body.'

Virkar placed his foot on Colasco's chest again. He was trying to feel the tiny electric currents he had felt when he had stomped on Colasco earlier. However, this time he didn't feel any tingling sensation in his leg.

'Get a doctor, quick!' shouted Virkar, as he fell on his knees next to Colasco.

'I've already called him, saheb. He's on his way,' said the young constable.

Virkar saw that the foam that was continuing to bubble out of Colasco's mouth was flecked with blood. Colasco was making incoherent guttural sounds. Virkar leaned closer to the man's ear and said, 'Mr Colasco, hold on, the doctor is on his way.'

But Colasco kept babbling. Virkar tried to make sense of his garbled words but couldn't comprehend anything. Suddenly, Colasco's right hand shot up and grabbed Virkar's shirt lapel. With surprising strength, Colasco pulled Virkar towards him until the Inspector was so close to that he could smell the faint odour of burnt flesh emanating from his body. Inaudible words streamed out of Colasco's mouth along with blood-speckled foam. Virkar strained his ears, trying to make sense of the man's garbled words. 'Please, could you speak a little louder?' he urged. Suddenly, he felt Colasco's hand going limp on his shirt lapel and dropping to the ground with a faint thud. His mouth had frozen in mid-speech and his glazed eyes had turned still.

A bespectacled man with a briefcase rushed towards Colasco along with a policeman. 'Doctor saab has arrived,' some people murmured in the crowd. The man knelt next to Virkar and immediately started giving Colasco a cardiac massage to try and revive him. Realizing that there was nothing more he could do, Virkar slowly raised himself to his knees. With drooping shoulders, he turned away from the futile ministrations of the doctor. Virkar suddenly felt drained as he stood surveying the crowd that was chattering in hushed tones.

Raashi and her cameraman came into his blurred vision. They had obviously been filming the entire episode as it had unfolded. Virkar searched Raashi's face for censure but was surprised to see her face displaying shock and dismay laced with sympathy. Perhaps that was the reason that, when she caught his gaze, she signalled her cameraman to turn the camera off. Before she could ask the inevitable question, Virkar offered, 'Colasco's last words sounded like, "hurry…tracing…tracing's ward".'

16

Barkat Alitronics was being stripped apart under the regretful gaze of its owner. The still-seething Virkar had found out that Barkat Ali was the man who supplied the mike and loud speakers every year to the Kunjupada event. A speedy visit to Barkat Ali's shop had resulted in what Virkar had expected: there was no sign of the suspect, now famously known as the Compass Box Killer. Rapid cross-questioning had revealed that a new recruit, a young man who called himself Ilyas and who resembled the police sketches of Nandu and the man who had posed as Sandesh Jejurikar, had not reported to work that day. Just one resounding slap on Barkat Ali's face had further revealed that Ilyas' first major—and as it turned out, last—task had been to install the mike and the loud speakers at Kunjupada the previous day. He had apparently carried out his duty diligently. Finishing late last evening, he had reported its completion over the phone before quitting for the day. But the next morning, Ilyas had called Barkat Ali on the phone and excused himself from work on account of running a temperature. After the tragedy at the Kunjupada's function, Barkat Ali had frantically tried calling Ilyas, but the phone had been switched off.

A visibly shaken Barkat Ali had then opened up the portals

of his workshop to the police who wasted no time in rounding up all the workers and individually interrogating them. But as usual they came up with nothing but a sketchy profile of the young man named Ilyas who had joined only a few days ago and had kept mostly to himself.

Having recovered by this time, Barkat Ali cursed Ilyas and spat out his paan. 'That bhenchod! I knew there was something satkela about him.'

Virkar shot back through clenched teeth, 'You knew that there was something wrong about him? Why the hell did you employ him then?'

'Arrey, Inspector saheb, where do you get good technicians these days? Everyone has gone to Dubai.' Barkat Ali emitted a rueful chuckle.

Virkar clenched his jaw even tighter. He was fed up of hearing how 'good' the killer was. He was fed up of always being one step behind the killer. He was fed up of people dying on him. 'Please tell your men to be a little gentle, Inspector saheb,' Barkat Ali's voice cut in through Virkar's thoughts. 'I have customers to please and a business to run!' The policemen were shoving things around as they sifted through the electronic goods lying on the repair tables. Suddenly, a small microwave crashed to the floor and broke into pieces.

'Saheb, please! The owner will take full vasooli from me,' yelped Barkat Ali. Virkar eyed the man without uttering a word. The crash of glass was heard from another corner. A policeman had dropped the glass top of a front-loading washing machine in his impatience.

Barkat Ali was near tears. 'Saheb, please, I will become kangaal this way!'

Virkar looked him squarely in the eye. 'I'm sure you earn

enough from your hawala business to avoid that.' The blood drained from Barkat Ali's face. He tried to get up from his chair.

'Sit down!' barked Virkar. 'My men are not looking for your hundis or other record books. They are looking for something that Ilyas would have left behind: a student's compass box. As soon as they find it, they will stop.'

Barkat Ali sank back into his chair. 'If I see that guy anywhere, I'll give him one solid punch kaan ke neeche...' he muttered to himself.

'Since when have you been supplying loud speaker systems to Kunjupada?' Virkar cut in.

'Saheb, why only Kunjupada? I've been supplying to akkha Dharavi for the past thirty years,' Barkat Ali said proudly.

Virkar frowned. 'Should I repeat the question?'

Virkar's icy tone had its effect. Barkat Ali's boastful tone suddenly grew meek. 'Saheb, I have been supplying to Kunjupada for the past five years. I don't charge the slum dwellers for this.' He paused and added, 'It's my social service for Colasco saheb.'

The realization that the killer had intimate knowledge of each victim and their activities suddenly hit Virkar. *He must have observed the victims closely for over a year.*

Virkar walked around the godown lost in his thoughts. *Why didn't the killer just buy a country-made pistol and shoot his victims on a dark night?* The answer came to him instantly. *Because his motive runs deeper than merely killing his victims. The killer wants to say something more critical; he's sending us a message.* Virkar wondered where the compass box fit into the picture, but this time the answer eluded him.

Suddenly, his phone rang. It was ACP Wagh. Virkar sighed. By now, the media must be done crucifying him. He ignored the call, in no mood to take a verbal reprimand from his boss who, till now, had cleverly stood on the sidelines and watched the spectacle unfold. He glanced at his men and saw that, even though they were busy taking apart all the electronic goods one by one, they had not even covered a third of the rambling godown. Virkar sighed again. This was going to be a long night.

He turned towards Barkat Ali who, having lost interest in the policemen, was now watching a rerun of an old mushaira show on a television mounted at the shop front. Virkar called out to him. 'Can you please change the channel to CrimeNews? I want to see the headlines.'

Barkat Ali shook his head. 'Saheb, this TV picks up only one channel: Doordarshan, my favourite.'

Virkar moved closer to the TV and peered at it in amusement. 'What's wrong with your TV? Why is there no colour?' he asked.

'Saheb this is my first TV; I bought it in 1980 when I got married. You won't believe it, it had not worked for so many years till that harami Ilyas came and fixed it. This is the only reason I gave him the job.' Then he went on to recount to Virkar how the upstart Ilyas had stunned him with his knowledge of electrical work, leading to Barkat Ali entrusting the boy with the installations at Kunjupada.

Virkar's eyes narrowed to slits as a thought struck him like a bolt of lightning. He got up and quickly walked towards the television. Grabbing it in both hands, he wrenched it out of the wall cabinet. An anguished cry rose from behind him. 'Saheb! Please…that television is one of my last memories of my dead wife. She preferred it even after I bought a colour TV,' pleaded Barkat Ali.

Virkar ignored the man's request and in one singular motion raised the television over his head and smashed it on the ground. The television broke to smithereens, scattering glass, metal and chrome all over the tiny shop front. The shocked Barkat Ali sputtered behind him as Virkar kicked the debris around, searching for something. And then Virkar saw it. Lying on a bed of crushed glass and taped to a piece of the broken picture tube was the object of his search: an old, worn-out student's compass box. Virkar picked it up with his handkerchief so as not to get his own fingerprints on it, even though he knew that he wouldn't find the killer's fingerprints on this one either. By now, all the policemen across the godown had heard the crash and had come rushing to the shop front. Virkar laid the compass box on the shop counter and opened it slowly. The policemen exchanged glances with each other in the pin-drop silence that followed.

This time, the words written in blood said: Three down. Now you'll have to work harder. Find the Smooth Operator before I get to him.

17

'Inspector Virkar's bravery in the face of danger needs to be praised,' pronounced Raashi on her TV show. The earnestness with which she said this was in sharp contrast to the combative attitude she had displayed all along. Shots of Virkar trying his best to save the electrocuted Colasco began playing on the screen. Raashi's admiring voice played over the visuals. 'Inspector Virkar displayed great presence of mind, despite the fact that he, too, could have succumbed to the electrical current. Unfortunately, the shock delivered by the mike proved too fatal for Nigel Colasco. Later investigations by Inspector Virkar revealed that it had been deliberately plugged into an amplifier that wasn't grounded properly. The electrical current that ran through the mike stand when it was turned on was too strong for any human to withstand, as can be seen by Colasco's charred palms.' Raashi paused for a minute to allow the visuals of a dying Colasco to play in a loop. He was babbling incoherently, 'Hurry…tracing…tracing's ward.'

Raashi reappeared on the screen, looking solemn and restrained. 'Those were Nigel Colasco's last words. He died shortly thereafter.' The camera caught a close-up of Virkar's frustrated and dejected face with Raashi's soft voiceover saying, 'Inspector Virkar has been trying his best to provide protection to the victims, but it appears as though the Compass Box Killer is too smart for the Mumbai police. I spoke to ACP Wagh of the Crime Branch and this is what he had to say...'

A stoic ACP Wagh sitting at his desk stared into the camera, his bloodshot eyes more a result of Old Monk than tireless hours spent at work. 'We will get this killer,' he thumped his desk. 'It's only a matter of time, but get him we will.'

Raashi's tone now turned conspiratorial, her blue contact lenses twinkling. 'Would you like to see what our committed ACP Wagh did next?' Her voice rose theatrically. 'We now bring you exclusive footage procured by our special sting operation cell.' The visuals on the screen now cut to grainy spy camera footage. ACP Wagh was still sitting at his desk but now facing Inspector Virkar who was standing across from him with only his profile visible on the screen. The angle of the visuals was such that could have only been shot through a small, hidden camera placed on ACP Wagh's desk.

'Saheb, I believe that there is some clue in Colasco's last words,' said Virkar.

ACP Wagh looked at Virkar with exasperation. 'What clue, Virkar? A dying man speaks some gibberish and you think it means something?'

'Saheb, I would like to investigate this further,' replied Virkar in a quietly confident tone. 'I will—'

ACP Wagh cut him off. 'Virkar, you will do no further investigation. You're off the case from now onwards.'

'But, saheb, I've also discovered another compass box and a new note that—'

Wagh cut him off with a chuckle. 'Virkar, tujha doka phirlaya kai? Have you gone mad? You keep finding compass box upon compass box but you're not able to save the people whose names are written on the notes inside.'

'But, saheb…' Virkar protested.

ACP Wagh raised his hand. 'When you were transferred to the Crime Branch, I had high hopes from you based on the reputation you had acquired in Gadchiroli. Even though you are new here, I handed a high profile case of the murder of a police officer to you because you were the only outsider—untainted by the internal politics and corruption in the Mumbai Police.'

Virkar interjected. 'But, saheb, you know that I'm still investigating it…'

ACP Wagh cut him off again. 'Virkar, have you forgotten our department's motto is *Sadrakshanaaya Khalanigrahanaāya*— to protect the good and to destroy the evil? What's the point of being a good investigator if you can't provide good protection?' Virkar fell silent but Wagh continued, 'Now, some activist-type has gone to the High Court and is demanding that the case be handed to another investigating agency: the State CID or the CBI. Thanks to you, we've been made to look like incompetent fools.'

Virkar opened his mouth to speak, but ACP Wagh did not let up. 'I'm sorry, Virkar, but you had your chance. It's out of my hands now. I have told the Additional Commissioner to hand over the case to a more experienced team to get quicker results.'

Virkar stood silent, looking expressionless.

ACP Wagh looked at him pointedly. 'What are you waiting for? You are dismissed. Please go and warm your chair.'

Virkar saluted ACP Wagh and left the room. The grainy footage quickly faded away and Raashi reappeared on the screen. 'So that was the Mumbai police—rather, ACP Wagh—admitting his inability to solve this case.' Raashi jabbed the air with her manicured finger. 'The most important thing now is to find out who is next on the Compass Box Killer's list. Whose name is on the note in the latest compass box that Inspector Virkar just admitted to having found? I asked this question to ACP Wagh on the phone and this is what he had to say...'

The screen showed ACP Wagh's mug shot and played his irritated response. 'What new compass box, madam? From where have you got this information?'

Raashi raised an amused eyebrow at the screen. 'The Mumbai Police has suddenly turned very uncooperative, as you can see. But, according to eye witnesses who were present at the time the latest compass box was discovered, the note inside it named the killer's next victim as the Smooth Operator.' Raashi paused dramatically. The programme's music score rose to create a feeling of dread. 'Smooth Operator,' she repeated slowly, as the screen faded to black.

Virkar raised the remote and switched off his television set. He let the remote drop with a clatter onto the ground. He was lying on the cheap Rexene sofa-set in his small tenement at the police quarters in Bhoiwada. He had been sprawled out on the sofa since his return from ACP Wagh's office, moving only once to switch on the television to watch Raashi's 9.00 p.m. show, *Crime Update*.

Virkar now rose from his position on the sofa and walked to the small corner that served as his bath area. Picking up a bucket full of water, Virkar he poured it over his head. The cold water splashed over his fully-clothed body, soaking him from head to toe and snapping him out of his dulled senses. Raashi had taken him by surprise tonight. The woman had guts! He had to hand it to the Hunterwali for pulling off the sting operation. Thank God he hadn't blabbed too much in ACP Wagh's presence. Virkar peeled off the wet clothes and dumped them into the now empty bucket. Grabbing a thin towel off the rack, he rubbed himself dry. Quickly taking the three steps required to reach the steel Godrej cupboard that stood on one side of the room, he opened it and took out fresh underwear, a light cotton shirt and jeans. Pulling them on and brushing his damp, short hair with his fingers, Virkar slipped on the only pair of casual shoes he owned. A sense of relief washed over him as he locked his front door and stepped out of his modest living quarters into the pleasant night air. Shedding his official garb always lightened up Virkar's mood. 'Kha, pee, kar anand, aaj raat ban ja Dev Anand,' he said to himself as he straddled his Bullet and revved it up.

18

One would assume that a bar would hardly attract any customers at a time when Mumbai's doodhwalas are delivering milk, paperwalas are delivering bad news and children are being roused awake by Mumbaikar parents preparing to face a new day in an unpredictable city. But the crowded tables and busy waiters inside Sunny Bar in the wee hours of the morning told an entirely different story. Located in the whimsical Cinema Lane behind Metro Cinema, Sunny Bar was one of the few bars in Mumbai that ran its business on the illegal, two-shift module. The evening-night shift catered to the general hard-drinking public whereas its special early morning shift operated behind closed shutters between 6.00 a.m. and noon, catering to workers who had just got off their night shift—die-hard alcoholics and other sundry morning liquor enthusiasts.

Virkar had discovered the bar by accident. It was while working on a case that involved surveillance of a scamster who was admitted as a patient at the nearby Bombay Hospital that he had chanced upon it. Early one morning, Virkar had seen the scamster emerge from the hospital gates and make his way surreptitiously through the back alleyways. Virkar had trailed the scamster and had seen him walking into a crumbling building that looked like it had seen better days. An inconspicuous signboard on the peeling walls read 'Sunny Bar'. After the scamster had gone back to his hospital bed, Virkar had visited the bar pretending to be a desperate alcoholic. The cracked and peeling paint on the walls and the low hanging bulbs covered with wide lampshades bathed the bar in darkness. The hard, wooden benches next to the worn laminate tables were seats that only the hardcore alcoholics would choose to linger on. And yet, Virkar had been quite amazed at the activity he had seen inside. He was ready to crack down on the bar till he noticed that they were serving Godfather Beer. It had been a long night for Virkar and, suddenly, his suppressed tiredness had welled up inside him, begging for a sip of his favourite beer. Shamefaced, Virkar had ordered a Godfather and sat down in the vacant corner of a table already occupied by two men who looked extremely sleep deprived. Sipping his beer, Virkar couldn't help but eavesdrop on the conversation between them. He gathered that they were out-of-towners, tending to their mother who was fighting for her last breath at Bombay Hospital. The men had apparently taken a quick beer break after a long night of uncertainty. They were due to head back to the hospital shortly, bracing themselves for the inevitable. Virkar had looked around the dimly-lit room and noticed other customers who were more content in the bar than the world outside. He had realized that, despite overtly breaking the law, Sunny Bar did actually cater to a needy clientele. Virkar had walked away from the bar that morning deciding to let it thrive while making a mental note to avail of its offerings sometime again when he was in need.

Today, as Virkar took assured steps towards Sunny Bar, the sky was breaking into dawn and the first chirrups of birds could be heard. At 6.30 a.m. that morning, twenty minutes after entering the bar, Virkar kept his glass mug down on the laminate-topped table. He had just finished his first bottle of beer. He glanced at the waiter who was standing expectantly beside him. As if by magic, the waiter produced another chilled bottle of Godfather from behind his back and, with a small flourish, popped open the cap, allowing the foam to trickle tantalizingly out of the bottle's mouth. He poured the golden liquid into Virkar's mug and placed next to it, a plastic bowl of crunchy chaklis and a bowl of fresh coriander and mint chutney. Virkar smiled. This was the cue for the waiter to make himself scarce and let Virkar mull over his drink.

As he took a sip of the precious liquid, a familiar female voice rang out in the room. It sounded totally out of place in the muted murmur of Sunny Bar.

'So, is this what you do in the mornings, Inspector Virkar?' Raashi looked down at him, an amused smile playing on her lips.

She looks very different from her TV show persona, thought Virkar as he took in Raashi's appearance. She was dressed in a pair of jeans and a smart but plain T-shirt. Her hair was tied up in a ponytail and her face seemed devoid of make-up. In the dim light of Sunny Bar, it looked like she wasn't wearing her sky-blue contact lenses. Virkar couldn't be sure, but her eyes looked dark and were shining.

He was at a loss for words. Raashi's sudden appearance and her amused smile made him feel like he had been caught with his pants down. He looked around and saw the grins plastered on the men's faces and heard some hushed sniggers. Whispered comments like 'Pakda gaya!' and 'Ab toh iski dandi gul!' were heard around the bar, adding to Virkar's acute embarrassment.

Virkar was still trying to compose himself when Raashi sat down across from him saying, 'Normally, at this time I do yoga, but maybe I should give this drinking-in-the-morning thing a try.' Virkar's glanced suspiciously at her sling bag and her hands. Noticing this, Raashi held them up and said, 'No spy cameras, Inspector. I'm here in an unofficial capacity.'

What is this Hunterwali after now? Virkar's mind was racing but he managed to maintain a deadpan expression. 'I'm off duty,' he said perfunctorily. Raashi nodded and added in a sympathetic voice, 'And also off the case, I know...'

Virkar's lips curled with sarcasm. 'Thanks to you, madam, thanks to you.'

'But I did say good things about you...'

Virkar's eyes bored through her. 'Yes, among all the bad things you said about the police department.'

Raashi flinched. 'I thought I was doing my job. As it turns out, I overstepped a line when I placed the spy cam in the ACP's office. The channel bosses have asked me to go on a long leave,' shrugged Raashi.

'Then what are you doing here? You won't get any sympathy or further information from me,' hissed Virkar.

Raashi blushed. 'I...I...followed you to...express my regrets. You're a brave man, and I'm sorry that my actions have caused you trouble. I'd like to make amends.' Her voice had a sincerity that was not lost on Virkar.

'Looks like following me has become your life's mission,' he retorted, looking her in the eye. The unflinching transparency with which she returned his searching look made something shift inside Virkar.

'Look, just give mere mortals like me a few moments of peace when we can drown our regrets.' He sat back, relaxing his tense muscles for the first time since he had seen her. Raashi lowered her eyes but made no move to leave. For a while both of them sat in silence. Finally, Raashi reached into her sling bag and pulled out a mini voice recorder. Virkar sat up and eyed her suspiciously. Raashi pressed a button and suddenly Colasco's dying words filled the air between them. 'Hurry...tracing...tracings ward.' Raashi lowered her voice and said, 'Like you, I believe that there is a clue in these words. I've played it over and over again, but haven't been able to come up with anything.' Raashi pressed a button and Colasco's words began playing in a loop. Virkar and Raashi bent their heads forward in complete concentration, listening to the muffled desperation in Colasco's voice. For a while Virkar didn't say anything, but noticing Raashi's earnestness, he finally spoke up. 'After watching your show last night, I realized I couldn't just step away from the investigation.' Raashi didn't say anything but the look in her eyes indicated that she wanted him to go on talking. Virkar cleared his throat. 'I went straight to Colasco's Slum Baalak Suraksha office and was there all of last night going through his papers and records trying to find anything that might be linked to his last words, but I didn't find anything useful.'

'I know,' said Raashi. Virkar threw her a sharp look.

'I've been following you all night; how else would I know that you were here?' She broke into a self-conscious grin. For a few seconds, Virkar held his stony stare but then broke into laughter himself. Virkar and Raashi laughed together and suddenly lapsed into an embarrassed, self-conscious silence.

Raashi spoke after a long moment. 'Look, now that another Crime Branch team is taking over the case, you can't officially speak to anyone, but if there is anyone or anything that you would like to investigate unofficially, let me do it for you.'

Virkar studied her eyes, which, as he had discovered that evening, were luminous brown. His gaze trailed along her unpainted mouth and the smooth texture of her skin. *Was this a trap?* He shrugged off the notion. The Hunterwali came across as genuine enough now. Virkar nodded. 'Okay, but right now I've got nothing. Maybe *you* can tell me what "Smooth Operator" means? Is it some kind of slang?'

Raashi replied in a heartbeat. 'The only "Smooth Operator" I know of is that old song by Sade.'

Virkar raised a quizzical eyebrow. 'Shaade? I've never heard of this singer. Does he sing playback for Hindi films?'

Raashi giggled. 'Sade is a *she*—a British singer from the eighties.'

Virkar face turned red with embarrassment. He cleared his throat. 'A female British singer? How can she be connected to our Compass Box Killer?'

Raashi shrugged.

Virkar continued to think out loud. 'Hmm…maybe the killer is not Indian. Perhaps the killer is an NRI? From the NGO files I saw at Colasco's office, I discovered that he was connected to many international aid organizations that regularly send foreigners and NRIs to Mumbai for volunteer work.' Virkar took out three hundred-rupee notes and slipped them under the beer mug. He gave Raashi a small nod and rose to leave.

'Hey, where are you going?' Raashi looked surprised.

'I'm going back to Colasco's office. I have to check out this NRI angle, I hadn't thought of it before. I probably have a couple of hours left before the peons come to open the office.'

Raashi clicked her tongue. 'Take it easy, Virkar, I was just showing off my knowledge of western pop music. How can you jump to conclusions based on an old song called *Smooth Operator?*'

Virkar turned to go. 'Maybe I *am* jumping to conclusions. But I've got to check out all the possibilities. I've overlooked too many things already and made too many mistakes.'

Raashi got up to join him. 'I'll come with you.' But Virkar put out a restraining hand. 'No, thanks. I'll do this on my own.' Raashi looked at him, a little miffed.

'Don't worry. If I find something, I'll definitely let you know,' he added, his tone reassuring.

Raashi attempted to protest as they walked out into the back alley that served as the exit for patrons of Sunny Bar's morning shift. But Virkar smiled at her and ducked into a narrow bylane where he had parked his Bullet. As he rode away, Raashi's face bore an indecipherable expression of concern and dread.

19

'Tracy Barton. That was her name. Tracy Barton from Durham, England. "Little Orphan Tracy". Taken in by abusive foster parents who cared less for her and more for drugs, an addiction that they both succumbed to when she was sixteen. Tough Tracy. Who had put herself through school and got herself the best college education through sheer grit and intelligence. She had landed herself a plum corporate job as soon as she graduated and was well on her way up, climbing the rungs of the corporate ladder, when suddenly, at the age of twenty-five, Tracy quit her job, left London and travelled to Indian shores—to Dharavi, Asia's largest slum in Mumbai, to be exact. Tracy planned to dedicate her life to orphaned children in India. She wanted to set up the biggest Adoption Agency in the UK. But first, she wanted to understand the way the system worked. After coming to India, she moved from one orphanage to another to try and understand the formalities that came with adoption in India. She travelled to nearby villages, helped out in blood donation camps, taught English in sundry literacy drives, cleaned slum drains till her hands were calloused, worked tirelessly for the underprivileged till her clothes carried the smell of her travels and her white skin turned a crisp brown under the harsh Indian sun. Her delicate looks, however, did not fade. Despite her dishevelled hair, her chipped fingernails smelling faintly of dried wood smoke, she was never short of attention from the opposite sex,' said the forty-something Lourdes D'Monte, Colasco's long-time private secretary.

She paused to take a brief respite from her outpouring and then continued, 'Tracy was such a good soul. She used to tell me that even while studying in London and working two jobs to pay her college fees, she managed to save enough money to send to India to sponsor the upkeep of orphans like her.' Lourdes' eyes turned moist. Loyal, God-fearing Lourdes who had been party to all of Colasco's secrets had remained mum all through the investigation. But now that Colasco was dead and Inspector Virkar had landed at her respectable, middle class home in C.G.S. Colony, Antop Hill, at an early morning hour, stinking of sweat and stale beer and scaring her two little children, Lourdes' tongue had let loose. 'Tracy first came in contact with Nigel Colasco when she met him during one of her many trips to the Mumbai slums. Later, she worked briefly with Slum Baalak Surakasha. Tracy was…'

Virkar, who had been listening to Lourdes patiently, suddenly cut her short, 'Was?'

After he had thought of the 'NRI/foreigner' connection to Colasco during his conversation with Raashi, Virkar had remembered seeing an email folder the previous night called 'International Contacts' in Colasco's inbox on his office computer. Virkar was desperate to join the dots. Colasco's last words had been echoing in his mind even though ACP Wagh had dismissed their significance. He had gone back to Colasco's office and picked the lock, as he had before, to quickly gain entry. At Colasco's table, Virkar had turned on the computer and hacked into Colasco's email account again by keying in Colasco's date of birth and month as the password. The fact that most people still foolishly used their date of birth or their mother's maiden name as their email passwords never ceased to amaze Virkar.

Having gained access to the 'International Contacts' folder, Virkar had typed out Colasco's last words, 'hurry', 'ward' and 'tracing' one by one in the search bar. The first two had yielded no results but as he typed T-R-A-C it had thrown up the name and email address of someone called Tracy Barton. Virkar discovered that, though the name did exist in Colasco's email address book, there were no email exchanges between him and Tracy. This could only mean that the emails between them had been deleted. His policeman's instinct had urged him to follow this lead, however slender it seemed to be. He quickly looked through all the files on the computer but found no emails or letters. Glancing at the filing cabinets lined up on one side of the office, he realized that he didn't have time to go through them. In any case, since he had already gone through them the previous night, he felt he wouldn't find anything. But Virkar wanted to dig deeper, which meant that he'd have to shake information out of someone. And he knew exactly who that person was. He had immediately ridden his Bullet to Lourdes' house. He was, in fact, quite taken aback at the ease with which he had managed to squeeze out information from Lourdes. He wondered if Tracy Barton could be *the* 'tracing' in Colasco's last words. Was he inching closer to finding the Compass Box Killer?

Now Virkar repeated his question. 'Why have you been using the term "was"?'

Lourdes raised a quizzical eyebrow in response.

'I'm sorry, I don't understand your question,' she replied.

'You keep referring to Tracy in past tense. Where is she now?'

asked Virkar, trying his best to remain patient.

Lourdes gave him a strange look. 'At the Christian Cemetery in Lonavala.'

Virkar felt as if someone had punched him in the gut. 'What... when...did she die? How?' Virkar managed to croak.

A tear rolled down Lourdes' cheek. 'She died in 2004 in a car accident in Khandala.'

Virkar sank back into the ratty old sofa. Suddenly, he felt tired. Very tired.

'Nigel sir was very shaken by the suddenness of her death. He couldn't bear to be reminded of her, so he deleted all her mails and photographs,' Lourdes added gently.

'Colasco was her...?' Virkar's mind struggled to focus as he tried to probe further.

'Her good friend,' replied Lourdes, her loyalty towards her deceased boss reasserting itself.

Virkar changed tack. 'Hmm... Where was Colasco when Tracy died?' he asked.

'Here, in Mumbai,' Lourdes stated. 'Tracy had gone on one of her solo weekend trips to Khandala, borrowing Nigel sir's car. She had drunk a lot of booze and fell asleep while driving. Later that night, Nigel sir was woken by a call from the Khandala police who told him that his car had been found at the bottom of a ghat with Tracy lying dead at the steering wheel.'

Virkar's policeman's instinct was completely alert now.

'How old was Tracy when this mishap occurred?'

'In her mid-twenties, I suppose,' replied Lourdes. 'Why?'

'A young foreigner drunk and dead in a car crash should have made headlines,' Virkar said, looking pointedly at Lourdes.

'It was 2004, sir, the news channels were not what they are today. It did make it to the newspapers, but as a small news item in the inside pages,' said Lourdes, without missing a beat.

Virkar made a mental note to check newspaper archives. 'What about her family? Didn't they come to claim her body?'

Lourdes now looked tired. 'Haven't you been listening to me, Inspector? Tracy was an orphan; she had no one in this world. Some of her friends sent a few condolence emails, that's all.'

'Why was Tracy driving drunk and alone at night?' Virkar asked, his fingers drumming against the sofa's armrest.

Lourdes looked at him blankly and shrugged. 'I… I never asked Nigel sir; he was so devastated.'

Virkar was not satisfied. 'But what about the police? Wasn't there an investigation?'

'Yes, of course there was one,' said Lourdes. 'The investigation declared it to be what it was—an unfortunate accident.'

With some effort, Virkar raised himself from the sofa that he was sorely tempted to make his bed. Thanking Lourdes and apologizing for his sudden appearance at her doorstep, Virkar walked out into the bright and busy street. It was 8.30 a.m. He turned his face up towards the sun, letting it warm his skin before getting on his Bullet and riding into the busy Antop Hill traffic.

His body was begging for some rest but his racing mind wanted him to ride straight to Khandala. To Tracy's grave.

20

Khandala

Up until the mid-noughties, Khandala and Lonavala, the small hill stations that lie on the Western Ghats of Maharashtra, perhaps ranked highest on a list of weekend vacation retreats in India, courtesy the weekend-warriors from Mumbai who mercilessly swarmed the twin hill stations for rest and recreation. The allure was such that, at one time, almost every self-respecting 'yuppie' from Mumbai aspired to own a weekend retreat on the green slopes of the ghats. Many of them did manage to fulfil their dream, leading to houses being built in droves and transforming Khandala and Lonavala from quaint, picturesque hill towns, to concrete-stricken, hilly suburbs of Mumbai. The twin towns' weekend charm fell on hard times as the average corporate Mumbaikar's disposable income increased and their travel ambitions soared. While the flushed-with-funds Mumbaikars began seeking solace in better climes, Khandala and Lonavala slowly became the holiday destination of the budget tourist from interior Maharashtra. As the breezy Mumbai-Pune Expressway eliminated the need to pass through Khandala and Lonavala while travelling between Mumbai and Pune, it is only the die-hard trekkers who make their way along the old Mumbai-Pune Highway to partake of Khandala and Lonavala's faded glory these days.

Virkar smiled to himself as he zoomed past the usual morning traffic of struggling trucks that were huffing and puffing their way up the winding Bhor Ghat section of the old Mumbai-Pune Highway. The workhorse Bullet engine ate up the arduous eight-kilometre Khopoli-Khandala stretch, climbing the height of 369 metres with the ease of a champion steed. Virkar's dark mood began to lift as his Bullet crested the stretch in record time. After leaving Lourdes' house, he had called the on-duty officer at the Crime Branch headquarters and reported sick. Then he had gone back to his tenement, showered, changed into a fresh pair of faded jeans and a T-shirt and quickly packed a small backpack for his trip to Khandala. Then he had ridden his Bullet to a nearby cyber cafe to find Sade's music video for *Smooth Operator* as well as archived Internet news reports on Tracy's accident. Twenty minutes later, he was back on his Bullet, making his way to the Eastern Express Highway leading out of Mumbai.

As he entered Khandala, Virkar mentally debated whether he should head directly to Tracy's grave at the Christian Cemetary in Lonavala or visit the Khandala police station first to look up old police reports on the accident. His cursory search of the Internet had yielded only a sketchy account of the accident and Virkar was curious to read its exact details. But he decided to first check into a hotel and change into 'sober' clothing befitting an Inspector from the Mumbai Crime Branch.

Virkar turned his Bullet into a winding bylane hoping to find his way to Katrak Villa, the old guest house that he used to frequent in his teens. Virkar and his friends would beg and borrow from their respective relatives for weekends filled with cheap liquor and hundreds of rounds of Mendicoat, their preferred gambling card game. To his delight, Katrak Villa still existed, looking almost the way it had when he visited it last, around fifteen years ago. Rustomji Katrak, the old Parsi owner had died and passed the ownership to his son, Pesi, who had decided to run the small guesthouse much the same way that his father had. Unfortunately, times had changed and people's desires had expanded, leaving Katrak guesthouse with only a few odd customers for the weekend. This suited Virkar just fine as he was able to take his pick of the rooms, and despite the dampness and the cracked walls, he chose the corner room he had frequented in his youth—it had the best view of the greenery surrounding the property. Changing into a simple full-sleeved shirt and cotton trousers, Virkar left for his destination, locking his room with the padlock provided by Pesi.

'Shinde saheb?' asked Virkar of the constable on duty at the Khandala Police Station. Even though Virkar was not in uniform, the constable saluted him. Policemen can always spot one of their own ilk because of the manner in which they carry themselves. Besides, the authority with which Virkar had spoken left no room for doubt that he was a policeman, and an officer at that. The constable got up respectfully and led Virkar to Senior Inspector Shinde's office at the back. As he entered the station, he surveyed the solid, whitewashed walls and the brick-and-tile construction of the old army barracks undoubtedly built during the British era to house the Indian soldiers who protected the vacationing British officers and their families. Senior Inspector Shinde's office was in a small hut at the back of the barracks that housed the main police station.

Outside the door that displayed the senior inspector's name, the constable halted in deference but Virkar brushed past him without breaking his stride. Pushing the door open, Virkar strode into the room. Inside, the stocky, bushy eyebrowed, dark-skinned Senior Inspector Shinde looked up, startled, a little annoyed at the interruption. His eyebrows shot up to the middle of his forehead.

'Shinde saheb, I'm Virkar.' He saluted smartly.

Shinde's eyebrows relaxed. A broad smile broke across his dark face. 'Ah, yes! Apte had telephoned me about you. Please have a seat.'

Virkar thanked him and pulled out a chair to sit down. Earlier, Virkar had made some enquiries and discovered that Inspector Apte, his police academy batchmate, had served with Shinde in the Ratnagiri district in coastal Maharashtra. Shinde banged his hand on a steel call-bell lying on the glass top of his desk. Almost immediately the constable's head popped in. 'Two special chais, phataphat,' Shinde ordered. Turning his attention back to Virkar, Shinde smiled again. 'Please tell me how I can help the Mumbai Crime Branch.'

Virkar cleared his throat. 'Uh…Shinde saheb, I'm here on an unofficial matter…' Shinde's eager voice cut Virkar in mid-sentence, 'Yes…yes…of course. But you are from the Mumbai Crime Branch, isn't it? It is not often that people like you come to meet forgotten policemen like us in Khandala.'

Virkar opened his mouth to speak just as his gaze fell on a large wooden signboard on the wall behind Shinde's chair. He froze. The signboard listed the senior police inspectors who had headed the Khandala Police Station over the years, along with their year of joining and leaving. Shinde's name had been freshly painted at the bottom of the list, giving his year of joining as 2010, but what had grabbed Virkar's attention was the name of one of the two predecessors above Shinde: 'Tukaram Akurle 2002-2004.'

21

The shifting seasons have made the Khandala and Lonavala hill stations prone to sudden cloudbursts right from June to late November. So it was not surprising that a light drizzle accompanied by a thin layer of fog had begun to make its presence felt by the time Virkar left the Khandala Police Station and got back on his Bullet. As his light cotton clothes turned damp while trying to make his way down the now slick slopes, Virkar cursed under his breath, wishing he had carried a windcheater along with him. Suddenly, a thought struck him and he pulled to an abrupt stop by the side of the road. Getting off, he lifted the seat of the Bullet and from the small cavity below, he extracted a folded plastic carry bag that he usually stashed there for such emergencies. Realizing that his palms were wet, Virkar rubbed his fingers on the seat of his pants, the only dry part left of his clothing. He then dug them into his right trouser pocket and fished out the slightly damp, folded sheets of paper on which were photocopied the Panchnama and police report of Tracy Barton's fatal accident along with her death certificate. He folded the plastic carry bag in such a way that it would become completely airtight and then, stuffing the package back into his trouser pocket, he swung his leg over the seat and gunned the Bullet back on to the road. By now the temperature had dipped a couple of degrees and the cold wind that swept past him made him shiver but it didn't stop him from making his way to the Christian Cemetery in Lonavala.

No one was in sight when he reached the locked iron gates of the cemetery. Virkar parked his Bullet outside along the stone wall that bordered the property. The watchmen had perhaps taken off to seek the comfort of their dry homes as soon as the drizzle began. He made his way into the cemetery by scaling the gate, all the while looking around for someone to come and stop him. But no one did.

Virkar let his eyes wander over the dense overgrowth that had obliterated most of the paths between the old, ornate European tombstones that stood in stoic silence...wet sentinels of days gone by. A rampant overgrowth of lilies, with droplets weighing down their petals, nestled over most of the graves, threatening to choke the life out of them. At the police station, Virkar had been told that the Protestant burial site was to the left while the Roman Catholic burial site was to the right, but he had no idea to which side Tracy belonged. Sighing to himself, Virkar started walked down the path to his right. He saw a number of European names—Ballard, Roberts, Smith—but didn't find the one he was looking for: Barton. Walking slowly, row by row, grave by grave, making his way through the wild lilies, Virkar kept searching. Suddenly, tucked away in a corner behind a large headstone that belonged to a nineteenth-century British gentleman named Charles Worthington, he found what he was looking for—an unkempt grave below a rotting wooden cross with an inscription that read: 'Tracy Barton (1976-2004)'.

Virkar stood at the foot of the grave and silently regarded the cross that seemed to have been hastily stabbed into the head of the grave. The drizzle had now soaked through his clothes but he paid it no heed. Instead, his mind wandered to the police report and death certificate which were firmly ensconced in the plastic carry bag in his trouser pocket. Virkar had studied these in detail earlier and, to his surprise, found that, while the police report was signed by Senior Inspector Akrule, the death certificate was signed by none other than Dr Prabhat Bhandari, the Compass Box Killer's second victim. The last sheet of paper that the eager-to-please Inspector Shinde had given him was the Morgue Release Sheet that certified that Tracy's body was released into the custody of a certain Nigel Colasco. Virkar had finally found the connection between Akurle, Bhandari and Colasco. But instead of being happy about his discovery, a sense of sadness had taken over him.

Virkar's thoughts were disrupted by the sound of distant footsteps. He turned around, startled, but only rows and rows of graves stared back at him. On seeing nothing except the fog and drizzle in the fast-fading light, Virkar dismissed the sound as that made by a twig snapping in the wind. Turning his attention back to the Tracy's grave, Virkar wondered if it would give him a clue as to why the three dead gentlemen, Akurle, Bhandari and Colasco, had conspired to do away with the kind-hearted young woman from England. And who was the Smooth Operator? Was he the fourth conspirator?

Virkar let the question boil inside him till he couldn't hold it in any longer. 'Who is the Smooth Operator? Tell me, Tracy, tell me!' he shouted into the rain that had started to pelt against his skin. The sound of his voice railing against the rain and the wind broke the spell. An embarrassed Virkar swiftly turned and began to find his way out of the cemetery.

As Virkar trampled his way towards the gate, the thin, dark

figure of the killer shrunk back ever so slightly into the main arch of the mausoleum that was situated at the back of the cemetery. Merging totally with the dark, wet, stone structure, the killer stood still, watching Virkar depart. He did not move until the roar of Virkar's Bullet faded into the distance. When the only sounds that could be heard were those of the raindrops falling on the lilies, the killer broke away from the shadows and silently walked towards Tracy's grave.

At the foot of the grave, he slowly lowered himself on to the ground at the same spot where Virkar had stood just a few minutes ago and stared at the engraving on the tombstone while the rain beat down relentlessly around him.

22

'Smoothy and I are leaving for a dirty weekend in Khandala, if you know what I mean,' laughed Tracy into the phone, making that gurgling sound deep inside her throat that always indicated her sense of mischief.

Listening to her on the other end of the line, he wondered if what Tracy had said was good or bad. And then he suddenly understood. His face flushed red, turning his ears hot with embarrassment. For a couple of seconds he froze, not knowing how to react. Flustered at his own reaction, he cut the line abruptly.

Tracy and he had been chatting as they usually did on Friday evenings. She had told him that she had just met her friend, Nigel Colasco, and was on the way to her apartment to get ready for her weekend trip with Smoothy. Weekends were sacred to her, coming from a culture that believed in worshipping the last two days of the work week. He never understood her obsession with the weekend, but she had explained that it was the only time that she seemed to be able to relax.

He stared at the mobile phone in his hands. Suddenly, the screen lit up as she called him back, just as he knew she would, asking why he had hung up abruptly. He let the ringtone jangle away; he was in no mood to talk to her again. He put the mobile phone down on his wooden desk and walked towards the ceramic basin that protruded from the wall in one corner of the room. He turned on the basin tap and splashed some cold water on his face. The heat immediately dissipated from his face. He grabbed the thin cotton sheet that performed the role of his towel, and wiped his face. He walked back to his desk and saw that he had received two more calls from Tracy, but he wasn't ready to call her back...yet.

It was now almost twelve years since he became aware of her presence in his life, but he had only got to know her personally in the past two years. He remembered the excitement with which he had awaited her arrival from Mumbai, how he had wept at the first sight of his angel walking through the gate towards him. She had come bearing numerous gifts, but the only gift he had wanted was a few precious moments in her company before she left for Mumbai again.

Tracy had returned to Mumbai the next day, but had kept in constant touch with him, assuming the proverbial role of his friend, philosopher and guide. His Godsend. Her tendency to use expletives and the occasional sexual innuendo were the only traits that bothered him. It went against his conservative Indian mindset. But she was perfect in every other way.

He had begun to share with her his deepest, darkest fears and found that she could relate to all of them. The ease with which she could pull him out of a bad mood only brought her closer. In turn, she spoke to him about her ideas, her vision, her dreams of alleviating the misfortune of the underprivileged children of India. She confided in him, seeking his opinions and valuing each one.

But lately she had been very distracted; her calls to him

had reduced in their frequency. He had guessed it was because of that man, the one she called Smooth Operator, or Smoothy. She had met him a couple of weeks ago at one of Mumbai's high society parties that her friend Nigel Colasco had hosted to attract contributions to his NGO. For a young, beautiful foreigner, partying was a sacred ritual—where all caution was thrown to the wind, inhibitions were shown the door, and mingling and mating were high on the agenda. At this particular party, she had been accosted by a suave young man who had walked up to her with a flute of champagne in his hand and a conversational skill that was as smooth as silk. In her defence, she had tried to maintain some semblance of propriety and sought to involve him in her life's mission to save the orphans of India. The Smooth Operator had listened attentively and then countered with his equally passionate opposing views. Anyone who knew of Tracy's deep-rooted commitment to her work would have thought that that would have spelled the end of their budding romance. But in hindsight, something in that conversation—or perhaps it was the champagne—worked for her and by the time the evening drew to a close, she had become almost besotted with him. After that day, most of Tracy's telephone conversations were peppered with references to the Smooth Operator, to the point that unnatural jealousy had begun to rear its ugly head inside his mind.

◎

A loud 'ding' had announced the arrival of a text message. He had grabbed the mobile phone to read: 'Sorry for making a silly joke. Still not used to our cultural differences. But you need to grow up too. Have a great weekend! ☺' The smiley seemed to mock him. Indignant heat prickled his ears, his knuckles turning white as he clenched the mobile phone in his hand, fighting the urge to send her a caustic reply. But he had managed to refrain from saying what he really thought of her vulgar jokes.

Unfortunately, she had not considered him close enough to seek his opinion on this Smooth Operator. When he had asked her why she called that man by that strange name, she had let out a flippant laugh and asked him to watch Sade's music video. When he had told her that he didn't understand what she was talking about—he hadn't heard of Sade—she had laughed again but offered nothing further. That was when he had decided to be honest with her. He had shared his misgivings about this Smooth Operator who seemed to be taking up so much of her time and pulling her away from her work and friends. But Tracy had brushed his doubts aside, telling him that he wouldn't understand her feelings even if she explained it to him. 'You are too inexperienced for matters of the heart.'

But he did understand the way she felt. He understood every bit of it.

Still on his knees in front of Tracy's grave, the killer felt his tears mix with the raindrops as they fell hard on the ground. He wished, as he had every single day since, that he had picked up his phone and called Tracy back that fateful night.

23

As Virkar rode from the Christian Cemetary to Katrak Villa in the rain, he kept trying to figure out why a police officer, a doctor and an NGO activist would conspire to cover up the car accident of a British woman in Khandala.

On entering his room, Virkar quickly stripped off his wet clothes and changed back into the faded jeans and T-shirt he had worn earlier that morning. He then headed for Pesi's living quarters in the outhouse of Katrak Villa to ask for directions to the nearest bar. He was advised to go to Pesi's favourite, the Ryewood Bar. Pesi was in a magnanimous mood and even lent him his old knee-length raincoat—the khaki-coloured, rubber-blended 'duckback' that went out of fashion a few decades ago. But it suited Virkar just fine, keeping him dry as he quickly made his way to the bar.

As was the case with many older establishments in the Khandala-Lonavala area, at 9.00 p.m. on a rainy night, the spacious confines of the Ryewood Bar were almost empty save for a smattering of people. The newer generation of visitors to Khandala and Lonavala yearned for excitement rather than rest and relaxation. They favoured the brightly lit bars equipped with

TV sets that blared non-stop Bollywood music from high-wattage speakers, drowning out any possibility of conversation.

Virkar entered the bar and sat on a stool in a corner. Opposite him, three white-haired pensioners were deep in conversation, discussing the intricacies of their LIC policies. At another table, a young couple whispered sweet-nothings to each other. A few tables away from them, a thin man wearing a floppy cricket hat that covered most of his face sat staring down at his glass. The only person who seemed to acknowledge Virkar's presence was the sleepy-looking barman, who looked as though he would do anything for the warm comfort of his bed at that moment.

Doctor's brandy with warm water was Virkar's choice that evening. As a young boy, Virkar had seen his father drinking copious amounts of it straight from the quarter-bottles. When he had enquired as to why his father drank the strong-smelling liquid, he had been told that it was medicine for his perennial cold, leading Vikar to associate Doctor's brandy with a cure for cold. It was only in his early twenties that he found out that brandy was a no-nonsense alcoholic beverage. The 'Doctor's' label was only a sales gimmick employed by marketers who wanted to give people an excuse to imbibe alcohol without guilt.

Virkar stretched his legs out in front of him and let the sharp liquid work its way down his throat. The brandy gave his body some warmth, but it was his soul that needed it more. He mulled over the reasons for his personal interest in finding out the truth about Tracy's death. During his decade-long career in the police, he had become used to death staring him in the face. But it was always especially difficult for him when the victim was a woman. Each time he heard or read about a crime against a woman, an inner voice would wish he had been there to protect the woman. He always shivered involuntarily when faced with the brutality of someone who had raised a weapon or otherwise snuffed the life out of a member of the gentler sex. He just couldn't get used to it, and somewhere deep inside, he didn't particularly want to.

Virkar's thoughts tumbled together as he worked his way down the brandy glass. Who would kill a kind, charitable woman like Tracy? Surrounded by the crime and corruption that was the part and parcel of a policeman's life, Virkar had always been in awe of those who could keep their life uncompromised—especially if it was to serve others selflessly without getting caught up in the trappings of power and prestige. And from what he'd heard from Lourdes, Tracy seemed to be that kind of a person. As a man of the law, he owed it to her to find the cause of her death, even if he was unsuccessful in catching the Compass Box Killer. Tracy had travelled all the way from Britain to Mumbai to help the unprivileged and yet someone had done her wrong. Virkar's mouth set in a thin line. He had made up his mind. He was going to get her justice, no matter how risky the journey was.

Virkar looked up from his empty glass and the barman's practised eyes connected with his. Before Virkar could react, the barman walked up to him with the steel peg-measure full to the brim. However, he poured only a 30 ml peg into Virkar's glass.

'How did you know I wanted a small?' Virkar asked.

The barman smiled. 'After three quick, large ones, your type normally switches to small pegs.'

Stung by the barman's words, Virkar tried to find a fitting reply but couldn't. Standing up, he pushed his bar stool back which scraped against the old wooden floorboards, making a loud sound. Except the thin man in the floppy cricket hat who seemed to be drowning in his drink, everyone in the bar turned to stare at him. Ignoring everyone's gaze, Virkar drew his wallet and extracted a slightly damp thousand-rupee note. He laid it on the bar counter, flung a dirty look at the barman and walked out of the bar into the drizzle. Once outside, he wore his raincoat, got on to the Bullet and rode out on to the narrow path that met the main road. Just as he turned a corner, the headlights of a car shone directly into his eyes, blinding him for an instant. 'Aai cha gho!' Virkar cursed as he stepped hard on his brakes and brought the Bullet to a sharp stop. He had narrowly avoided a collision. Gearing up for an argument, Virkar got off his Bullet.

'Had one too many, Inspector?' a familiar voice called out from the driver's seat and then broke into peals of laughter. Virkar stopped in his tracks. Now that the car's headlights were switched off, he could see the figure sitting at the steering wheel. Raashi.

'Judging by your expression, one would think you're not too happy to see me,' she said, dissolving into a fresh fit of giggles.

Virkar could only manage a self-conscious, 'I…uh…uh…'

'It's okay, Inspector. I'd be just as surprised as you are had you suddenly appeared in front of me like this.'

Virkar finally managed a slurred question. 'What are you doing here?'

'I've come to help you, of course!' Raashi grinned. 'You're a hard man to find, though. I looked for you in over twenty hotels till I got to Katrak Villa. Pesi was kind enough to guide me here. I was just heading to the bar to join you.'

Virkar stood in the middle of the road, shifting from one foot to the other, not knowing how to react.

Raashi noticed his discomfort and asked teasingly, 'So, are we going to continue talking like this in the open, or should we head to the bar?'

Virkar hesitated. 'Uh…I don't… There is no place inside. It's packed.'

Raashi nodded and turned the key in the ignition. She started backing up the car. 'No problem, Inspector. I've taken a room at Katrak Villa too.' She paused and added, 'We can either talk in my room or in yours. You decide.' She stepped on the accelerator and expertly reversed the car down the path and on to the main road. Virkar was left standing in the dark with only his Bullet for company and the buzz of the three and a half pegs of Doctor's brandy rapidly disappearing from his system. He stood motionless for almost a minute, debating his next move. Then, straddling the Bullet, he fired up the engine and muttered under his breath, 'Bhagwan jab deta hai, toh thappad kaan ke neeche deta hai.'

As the tail light on Virkar's Bullet receded down the darkened path, the killer emerged from Ryewood Bar and took off his floppy cricket hat from his head. Folding it up and shoving it into his trouser pocket, he began to walk towards the main road.

24

'He's killing me,' flashed the message in front of his half-shut eyelids. He picked up his phone and read the text that had woken him up in the wee hours of the morning.

This has to be another one of her stupid, flirtatious jokes, was the first thought that popped into his groggy head. He let the phone slip out of his fingers and on to the bed. Turning, he snuggled into his blanket and let himself slip back into its warm cosiness. As sleep overtook him again, he wished Tracy would see reason and get over her obsession with the Smooth Operator.

◉

The killer snapped out of his reverie; the events of that fateful night in 2004 never stayed far from his mind. *Be careful what you wish for, just in case it comes true*, thought the killer as he walked along the six kilometres of dark highway that stretched between Khandala and Lonavala. He was careful enough to walk in the trench that ran along the highway so that he wasn't in the direct path of any oncoming vehicle, especially one whose driver was drunk. The clouds that had brought the insistent drizzle earlier in the day had passed by now, leaving the moon to light his path. The wind blew cold against his face as his mind wandered back to the morning after he had received that text message from Tracy.

That day, he had slept almost until noon. Feeling hot and dehydrated when he had finally woken, he had reached for the bottle of water on his bedside table. As the cool water gushed down his throat, he remembered Tracy's text from the previous night. He still didn't believe her text had meant anything serious but feeling a little regretful about not having returned her call, he decided that Tracy had been ignored enough. He groped around his bedsheets and found his phone. Bracing himself for Tracy's anger, he pressed the return call button.

'This phone is out of coverage area,' the recorded voice informed him. He tried her number again after a few minutes, only to get the same automated message.

'She's probably picnicking on some hilltop with her blessed Smoothy,' he had muttered to himself.

However, a strange uneasiness niggled at the back of his head. He tried her number throughout the day and got the same response. By early evening, he began to grow restless. He started thinking of all the possible ways that he could get in touch with her in Khandala. Soon, he realized that he had no other option but to contact the Smooth Operator. But he didn't know anything about this man bar the nickname Tracy had given him. He wondered if this man was well-known in Mumbai's social circles as the Smooth Operator or if it had solely been Tracy's nickname for him. He wished for the umpteenth time that he had asked Tracy for the man's real name. But no, he had been too busy sneering at her liason with him to do so.

He rushed to a nearby cyber cafe and searched for 'Smooth Operator' on the Internet. He only came up with several listings for the pop song, *Smooth Operator*, sung by a British musician called Sade. Frustrated, he then searched the Internet for Tracy's friend, Nigel Colasco. He was the one who had introduced Tracy to the Smooth Operator. There were a few people listed under that name, but only one matched the kind of professional profile that Tracy had spoken of. Luckily, he found the phone number of Colasco's NGO. He then headed to the nearest STD booth and called the number. Three rings later, the phone was picked up by a peon. After two minutes, though, he hung up, having been informed that Colasco was out of town on some urgent business. Apparently, some friend of his had borrowed and crashed his car in Khandala. A knot formed in his stomach. He instantly knew that something was very, very wrong.

The following morning, he packed a bag and made his way to the train station. He bought himself a ticket to Lonavala and, while waiting for the train to arrive, he bought every possible newspaper at the A. H. Wheeler stall. Sitting on a bench in one corner of the railway platform, he rifled through every page, hoping against hope that he would not come across any bad news. But buried deep within the inner pages of the *Times of India*'s Mumbai edition was a small report that reported that a British woman called Tracy Barton had died in a car accident in Khandala two nights ago.

◎

By now, the killer had reached a ridge next to the highway that jutted out over the valley between the ghats. He walked up to the edge of the ridge to the point where the earth suddenly disappeared, creating a steep fall of about 200 metres. A familiar knot of fear began to form in his stomach as he thought of the day he had last stood there in 2004, trying to look down into the valley to spot the exact point where Tracy's airborne car had met the valley floor.

25

A thin ray of sunlight broke through the thick foliage outside Virkar's window and fell directly on his shut eyelids. Feeling the heat, he opened his eyes, only to flinch when the unrelenting beam hit his corneas. Rubbing his eyes, he sat up and looked around the room, heaving a sigh of relief when he saw that he was alone…and still fully clothed. He raised himself off the bed and walked into the attached bathroom. Peeling off his clothes, he stood under the shower as the memory of last night came flooding back to him.

Raashi was waiting outside his room when he had reached Katrak Villa on his Bullet. Realizing that there was no getting away from her, he unlocked his door and opened it to the embarrassing sight of his wet clothes and underwear drying on a chair kept right under the ceiling fan. Excusing himself, he quickly transferred his wet clothes to the towel rack inside the bathroom. When he returned to the bedroom, he saw Raashi sitting on the same chair with the now familiar amused expression on her face—an expression that never failed to annoy him.

Suddenly, she became business-like. 'Your colleague, Senior Inspector Sonavane, is quickly moving forward with the investigation,' she ventured. 'He has already arrested three different men who match the description of the Compass Box Killer and is interrogating them. He is sure that one of them will turn out to be the actual killer.'

The last part of her sentence was said with a raised eyebrow, as if wanting Virkar's concurrence. Virkar didn't say anything, staring at the rain-lashed night through the window as he sat across from her on the edge of his bed.

'So what have you found here...in Khandala?' Raashi finally asked.

Virkar remained silent.

Raashi sighed. 'Look, Inspector, I've already told you that whatever you share with me is off the record. I...I...just feel very guilty about how my reports affected you. I really want to help.'

Virkar looked directly into Raashi's luminous brown eyes. *Thank God she isn't wearing her blue contacts tonight.* He had always wondered why she wore blue contacts when her eyes were a naturally beautiful colour. Gazing at her intently, he realized that there was something different about her today. There was no rebuke or sarcasm written on her face. Rather, he saw something he had not seen before—an earnestness that led him to believe that what she was saying must be genuine. Mentally debating how much to share with her, he began to speak. Hesitant at first, he slowly opened up and soon, his thoughts and theories began to flow freely as he told her everything—how Akurle had been the policeman in charge of Tracy's case, how Dr Bhandari was the doctor who had signed Tracy's death certificate and how Nigel Colasco was the man who had buried her in the ground. He told her about his theory of the conspiracy hatched by the three men to make Tracy's death look like an accident. Virkar added that he felt the conspiracy could have been hatched at the behest of the fourth conspirator, namely the Smooth Operator.

And, of course, the possibility that the Compass Box Killer might have been a hidden fifth conspirator—one who had been a part of the cover-up earlier but had later decided to go against his co-conspirators. Perhaps someone unknown to the dead men, otherwise they would have tried to stop his killing spree. But why after nine long years? Why not earlier?

Raashi listened to him patiently and then asked him a simple question: 'Have you checked the hospital ward where Tracy's body was kept? Maybe Colasco was trying to tell you that the clue to the conspiracy lies in that ward?'

Virkar reacted as though he had been struck by lightning. 'Aai cha gho!' he cursed under his breath for not having thought of a clue that had been staring him in the face. He rose to his feet and gave Raashi a firm handshake, thanking her profusely. He wanted to find that hospital as soon as he could.

But his body suddenly refused to comply with him. His journey to Khandala, the events of the day and the three and a half pegs of Doctor's brandy had all taken their toll on his body. He sat back down on the bed, feeling tired to his bones and completely drained of energy.

'You need to rest,' Raashi said as she got up and made her way to the door. She turned to look at him one last time and broke into a wide smile. For the first time since he had met her, Virkar could not interpret the attractive crime reporter's expression and the slight dilation of her pupils. What she said next only increased his confusion. 'Well, Inspector, I hope you're not so tired tomorrow.'

And leaving him with that thought, she left the room. Virkar slumped back on his bed, allowing sleep to overtake his senses. He didn't remember anything after that.

Now, as he turned off the tap and reached for his clothes

drying on the towel rack, he decided to deal with the reporter later as there was a potential lead to be followed and he had no time to lose. Grabbing his wallet and his motorcycle's keys, he walked out of the door, crossed the veranda and headed towards the small parking compound.

But just as he entered the area, his feet came to a sudden stop. Raashi was casually leaning against her car, texting on her mobile phone. She looked up at him with a broad smile.

'Good morning! Shall we take my car, Inspector?' she asked.

'I…I…don't…' Virkar fumbled for words.

But Raashi cut him off. 'You weren't thinking of going alone, were you?' She threw him a challenging look.

Virkar tried to evade the question. 'I…I first have to find out where Tracy's body was kept.'

'At the Government Hospital in Khandala; they have a small morgue there,' she replied immediately.

Smiling at Virkar's flabbergasted expression, Raashi added, 'Uff oh, Inspector, you think you're the only one with investigative abilities? I've been up since dawn, making a string of phone calls.'

Virkar realized that he had lost the battle, but he was not going to lose the war. 'I only travel by my Bullet,' he said, taking brisk steps towards his bike. As he mounted it and turned the key in the ignition, Raashi flashed him the same enigmatic smile she had the night before. In a flash she was next to Virkar's Bullet, swinging one leg over the back seat as she straddled it. Placing a soft hand on Virkar's shoulder, she said, 'Ready to take me for a ride, Inspector?' The confusion rose in him once again, but this time it was mixed with the embarrassment that made blood rush to his ears. To cover it up, Virkar accelerated the Bullet and roared out towards the main road.

26

'Tracy Barton? Ah, yes, I remember her. An unfortunate accident case that occurred in…2003…no, 2004. The body was shattered from head to toe…very sad!' said Dr Tupe, the chief of the government hospital, letting the corners of his mouth droop. Something in his bulbous eyes, however, didn't read right to Virkar. Raashi and he were sitting opposite the doctor in his small office chamber at the Khandala Government Hospital.

'Was her body kept in a ward before she was moved to the morgue?' asked Virkar, looking around the small room whose walls were adorned with medical diagrams and duty charts. 'Were you on duty that night, Dr Tupe?'

The doctor straightened his reed-thin body in his chair and scrunched his middle-aged forehead, as if trying to get his eyebrows to meet his receding hairline. His frog eyes stared into the distance while Virkar studied him closely. Finally, when he stirred, Virkar concentrated on Dr Tupe's body language rather than his words. 'As far as I remember, she was declared dead on arrival and taken straight to the morgue,' said the doctor, blinking his eyes rapidly and scratching his head. 'Tch…so beautiful, so young…her face was smashed beyond recognition.' He shook his head a little too vigorously at the last bit.

He's definitely hiding something, thought Virkar as he sipped the tea served to him by an orderly. Virkar looked around the cramped room as if there were hidden clues calling out to him. He replayed the events of the morning in his head.

As a result of Raashi's early morning phone calls, Dr Tupe had been expecting them when they had arrived. 'I was surprised to hear about your documentary film on dead bodies. We don't get many dead people in Khandala,' he had smiled as he shook hands with them.

Virkar had caught on to Raashi's lie and glanced at her from the corner of his eyes.

'Thanks for agreeing to meet us at such short notice, Dr Tupe,' she said, suppressing a smile. 'Well, the documentary film is more about the history of dead bodies in old morgues.'

Dr Tupe's smile widened. 'Oh, yes! Now I understand. Our morgue is very old. Established during the British era. They loved to come and die here.' Raashi flashed him a broad smile acknowledging his dark joke. He smiled back, pleased with himself. This was probably the closest the doctor had ever got to celebrity, however minor, in his staid existence in Khandala, Virkar thought to himself.

'Um…can we take a look at it? The morgue?' Raashi asked.

'Sure, sure…no problem.' Dr Tupe then led them to the small morgue at the back of the hospital.

Outside the morgue, a khaki-clad man was lounging on a wooden bench, smoking a beedi. 'This is Bhoir, our morgue attendant,' said the doctor. Although a sudden visit by the chief of the hospital should have surprised him, Bhoir casually stubbed out the strong-smelling beedi. Placing the stubbed end carefully in his uniform shirt pocket, he continued to sit on the bench by the entrance as if he had no visitors in his midst. 'Bhoir has been here for over twenty years. Not many people want to work in a morgue, even if it is in a beautiful place like Khandala.' Dr Tupe smiled, but this time Raashi didn't smile back at his limp joke, causing the doctor to self-consciously clear his throat. 'I'll be in my office. Please join me for a cup of tea later,' he said, excusing himself and leaving them in Bhoir's care.

Bhoir reluctantly rose to give them the grand tour of the bare fifteen feet by fifteen feet room, where there was not much to see except old metal stretchers with large aluminium trays lying by their side. 'For keeping ice slabs. We don't have ACs,' he explained, noticing Raashi's curious expression. In a corner lay an old, body-sized freezer connected to a portable generator. It looked as if it had been modified from a freezer discarded by an icecream shop. Pointing at it, Bhoir spat out, 'That's for the VIPs.'

Virkar used this as a conversation starter. 'So, have you seen many dead VIPs in your twenty years here?'

Bhoir gave him a laconic smile. 'Just about two or three, saheb. VIP tourists don't stay in Khandala long enough to die.'

Virkar ignored Bhoir's attempt at replacing his boss as the resident joker and asked, 'Seen many foreigners?'

'A few,' Bhoir shrugged.

'What about a foreign woman? About nine years back? Tracy Barton?'

Bhoir's expression suddenly became guarded. 'Mala kahitari mahiti nai, saheb, I don't know anything,' he said while reaching for the beedi in his pocket, lighting it quickly and clamping it between his teeth, signalling the end of the morgue tour. But Virkar continued to walk around the morgue, poking into its nooks and crannies. He didn't find anything but he kept at it till a call from Dr Tupe had made it impossible to continue without being absolutely disrespectful to his host.

Now, as they sat sipping tea in Dr Tupe's chamber, Virkar was determined to find out what he and his morgue attendant were hiding. He decided to dispense with the niceties and come straight to the point.

'So, Dr Tupe, you knew Tracy Barton before she died?'

Dr Tupe blanched. 'No, no, I didn't. I didn't know her at all, but I… The first time I came to know of her was when they brought in her body.' He licked his lips and his gaze slid away, refusing to meet Virkar's.

'Hmm…so how did you ascertain that it was her if her face was unrecognizable?' asked the Inspector, starting to enjoy the doctor's obvious discomfort.

Dr Tupe opened and shut his mouth like a fish gasping for water. 'I… It was a long time ago. I don't remember what our staff doctors did nine years ago to establish her identity.' He fell silent but realized that Virkar was not satisfied with his response.

Raashi, who had been silent until now, spoke up. 'So you don't really know too much about Tracy's case?'

Somewhat relieved, Dr Tupe turned to her. 'Yes, you're right. I was only the deputy then, and all the high profile cases were handled by my boss, Dr Bhandari.'

Virkar raised an eyebrow. 'Dr Prabhat Bhandari?' He shot a glance at Raashi who returned his look with a non-committal shrug.

'Yes, he personally performed the postmortem on Tracy Barton's body,' said Tupe, relieved at the change in the line of questioning.

'Do you know that Dr Bhandari was recently killed in Mumbai?' Virkar asked, looking at him pointedly.

'Yes,' nodded Dr Tupe. 'Very sad!' Suddenly realizing that this was the same way he had reacted to Tracy's death, he looked away sheepishly and began to shuffle some papers on his desk. It was an indication to his visitors that he had other things that demanded his attention than a nine-year-old case of a foreigner who had died in Khandala.

But Virkar didn't back down. 'Do you think Tracy Barton's accident and Dr Bhandari's death could be linked?'

A thin layer of sweat had begun to form on Dr Tupe's forehead, but he replied in a steady voice, 'I'm just a local doctor who got a job in this hospital by chance. I'm only interested in doing my job and going home, sir. I wasn't even interested in becoming the chief here till Dr Bhandari resigned from government service and set up his own practice in Mumbai.'

'How long ago was that?' Virkar asked.

'Around nine years ago.'

Virkar lowered his voice to a menacing tone. 'Tracy Barton died around nine years ago—don't you think that's a strange coincidence?'

Dr Tupe now pulled himself together. 'Look, what's all this about? I was told that this was an unofficial visit about a documentary film on old morgues...' He glanced at Raashi for confirmation but she was busy observing her nail polish.

Virkar nodded and rose from his chair. 'Thank you, Dr Tupe. You've been very helpful...with the research on our doc.' The joke was not lost on his host who gaped but extended a limp and clammy hand towards Virkar who shook it firmly. Raashi, too, got up, slightly surprised by Virkar's sudden decision to leave. She followed him out of the room.

The Khandala Government Hospital lay on a small hillock overlooking the picturesque valley below with a spectacular view in all directions. But on the way to his parked Bullet, all Virkar could think of was how he could extract the information he was sure Dr Tupe was hiding.

Raashi, who had been walking next to him looking thoughtful, finally said, 'So, this was a dead end. Now what?'

Virkar started the Bullet. 'Now we shall have brunch,' he said, signalling her to climb on to the back seat.

27

The Chicken Satellite Sizzler crackled in front of Raashi, reflecting her volatile mood. Virkar and she were seated at a table on the terrace of the open-air Monkey Hill Restaurant. From their vantage point they had a spectacular view of the hillside that they had made their way down from. In front of them lay the lazy stretch of road that wound all the way back up to the government hospital. The Monkey Hill Restaurant was known for its spicy sizzlers as well as for the monkeys who frequented the terrace for scraps of food. In fact, the restaurant had shut down for a couple of years because a monkey had bit a lady while she was lunching. It had only reopened because the new management ensured that well-equipped attendants sporting thick bamboo sticks kept the macaques at bay while the patrons partook of their meals. Virkar had brought Raashi to the Monkey Hill Restaurant promising to review their visit to the hospital, but all he had done since they had taken their seats was to discuss the menu in depth! Every time Raashi tried to broach the subject of the hospital, Virkar quickly sidestepped the issue.

As the sizzle on her plate died down and the Chicken Satellite cooled down enough to eat, Raashi brought it up once again. 'So…what's your verdict on Dr Tupe?

In response to her query, Virkar picked up a few French fries drenched in melted cheese and pepper sauce. Popping them into his mouth, he masticated slowly, savoring the succulent juices as if they were tantalizing his palette.

Raashi's mouth twitched impatiently at the corners. She expressed her frustration by stabbing a still sizzling piece of chicken hard with her fork. But her action only drew a placatory response from Virkar; between mouthfuls, he spoke a muffled sentence that sounded like, 'We'll speak after we finish eating.' He picked up the fork and knife and began to cut a piece of his sizzler with the extra caution common among people who are uncomfortable using cutlery. A small smile of amusement crept to the corner of Raashi's mouth. She picked up her fork and knife and sliced her chicken steak with the ease of an expert. She saw Virkar following her hand orchestrations with interest. As his eyes connected with hers, a hint of embarrassment rippled across his face. Raashi popped a small piece of the chicken in her mouth, enjoying her victory, however small it was.

Virkar, in fact, was not looking at her but at something moving far away along the winding road that lay in front of them. While Raashi enjoyed her meal, Virkar peered over her shoulder at the moving object that turned out to be a man riding a bicycle. He smiled on seeing the approaching figure. All of a sudden, he spat out the contents of his mouth into his plate, making a loud belching sound.

'Eww...!' said Raashi and shrank back in her chair. She threw Virkar a disgusted look and sprang away from the table.

'I'm so sorry,' Virkar apologized, grabbing his plate and handing it over to a waiter. 'It must be because of that brandy I drank last night; I had a feeling it wasn't good.'

Raashi shrugged and said nothing but Virkar knew that she

was repulsed by his uncouth upchucking.

Virkar got up, looking embarrassed. 'Please excuse me while I visit the washroom.' Clutching his stomach, he rushed towards the men's toilets at the back of the restaurant. Watching him go, Raashi signalled the waiter to take her plate away too and asked for a coffee instead. She had lost her appetite.

Meanwhile, Virkar had walked past the gents toilets and exited through a small door that led to the back of the restaurant. He quickly crossed a small compound, heading towards the barbed wire fencing that separated it from the forest land along the hillside. He ducked through a gap in the barbed wire and made his way through the trees that lay beyond. Virkar soon found himself on one side of the winding road. Positioning himself behind a grassy mound that hung just above the road, he waited, watching the road. A few minutes later, the same cyclist came into Virkar's line of vision. He tensed. Waiting till the cyclist was right below the grassy mound, he jumped and landed on top of the rider, who lost his balance and fell hard on the road. Before the man could figure out what was happening, Virkar dragged him by the scruff of his neck behind the grassy mound. Leaving him lying there still dazed, Virkar ran back on to the road, plucked the fallen bicycle off the road and hid it behind the grassy mound, away from the prying eyes of nosy onlookers.

The cyclist was now coming to his senses. Virkar sat down in front of him and said in a low, menacing tone, 'Bhoir, now tell me what you know about Tracy Barton's body. You've got two minutes before I drag you and your cycle across to the other side of the hill and throw you into the valley.'

Bhoir began to stammer. 'Pl—please, saheb, I was not a part of it. I was ju—just paid 25,000 rupees to keep my mouth shut.'

The menace in Virkar's voice grew. 'You have one minute to

open that shut mouth.'

Bhoir swallowed hard. 'Someone strangled her with their bare hands after sex, saheb,' he half-whispered, unwilling to meet Virkar's gaze.

'Was she raped?'

'No, it wasn't forced sex.'

'Who told you that?'

Bhoir hesitated, but Virkar's resounding slap across his cheek got him talking again. 'Dr Tupe told me. He was on duty when they brought in the body. While they were busy doing the paperwork, he quickly examined the body.'

'Who are "they"? What paperwork?' barked Virkar.

'Inspector Akurle and Dr Bhandari, saheb. They brought her in and prepared the accident report.'

'What happened then?'

'I was called in. I stored the body in the VIP freezer. The next day, some Christian man called Colasco came from Mumbai and took the body away. I don't know where.'

Virkar was quiet for a few seconds, letting the information sink in.

'Please, saheb, I'm a poor man,' begged Bhoir, falling at Virkar's feet. Tears streamed down his cheeks. 'Tupe saheb and I were forced to take part in it. We were threatened and told to keep our mouths shut. They promised to take care of us if we did. They kept their promise. Tupe saheb got the chief's job and I got my 25,000 rupees.' Bhoir paused and added in a low voice, 'I'll return the money to them if you tell me to.'

Virkar stood up and brushed off Bhoir who was still clinging to his feet. 'Bhoir, you can go now. If you tell anyone about this conversation, I'll come to your morgue and lock you alive in your VIP freezer, understood?'

Virkar turned and ran into the foliage. Making his way through the barbed wire, he went back to the gents toilet. He quickly splashed water on his face and wiped himself down with a hand towel. Feeling pleased that everything had gone according to plan, he turned to head back to the terrace. Suddenly, he noticed a small tear in his cotton pants near his knees. The sharp edge of the bicycle pedal had nicked him as he had jumped on Bhoir, opening up a bloody gash. 'Aai cha gho!' Virkar swore as he dabbed the wound with some toilet paper and then made his way to the terrace.

Raashi looked at her watch as she saw him approaching. 'It's been twenty minutes since you've been gone! Hope...umm...your stomach is not giving you too much trouble.'

Virkar suddenly remembered his 'throwing up' incident and went red in the face. 'Ah, no, no. It's all right, thankfully. I'm sorry to have kept you waiting. I...umm...fell in the toilet. The floor was slippery.' He showed her his wound.

'Oh dear, that needs to be taken care of,' said Raashi, looking at him with concern.

'It's okay. Let's head back to Katrak Villa. I'll get some first aid there.'

He gestured towards the waiter.

'No worries, I've already paid the bill,' said Raashi. 'I'm ready to leave.'

'Then let's do that,' said Virkar, leading her off the terrace towards his Bullet. As he rode past the grassy mound, Virkar scanned the surroundings and smiled to himself. Bhoir was nowhere to be seen.

28

'Ahh!' The tincture of iodine stung badly as Raashi dabbed it on to Virkar's wound with a cotton swab. Virkar cursed Pesi Katrak under his breath for handing the tincture of iodine to Raashi as the best solution for wounds. As with everything else in Katrak Villa, the medicines in its first aid kit were also frozen in time. The world had moved on to soft, soothing antiseptic Band-Aids while people like Pesi were still using the dark liquid favoured by their grandfathers.

Raashi dabbed the solution on to the wound one final time and then dumped the bloody cotton swab into a dustbin. As she began to tidy up, Virkar sat up on his bed, watching her. He was feeling foolish sitting in a pair of old cargo shorts borrowed from Pesi. Raashi had assumed the role of his nurse and insisted that his wound needed to stay open while being treated. Since the only other garment he had was a pair of full-length jeans, he had used this as a convenient way out to refuse her treatment. But when she began to throw around words like 'septic' and 'tetanus', he had reluctantly agreed to play the wounded soldier and had ended up wearing Pesi's cargoes, since it was either that or his underwear.

Having finished playing nurse, Raashi dragged the wooden chair towards the bed, placing it as close as possible to where Virkar was reclining. She sat down squarely and faced him.

'So, Inspector. Are you going to tell me what Bhoir said to you?' she asked with a straight face.

Virkar didn't have time to be stunned as Raashi continued almost in the same breath, 'Just how many times are you going to test my skills, Inspector?'

Virkar felt a grudging admiration for her building up inside him. *She's good. Almost as good as me. But, how did she...?*

As though reading his mind, Raashi showed him the pair of compact pocket binoculars that she had taken out from her purse and he immediately understood. 'After you left, all I had to do was to use this little baby to spot Bhoir on his bicycle and I knew where you had gone. When you came back with your wound...' Raashi gave an all-knowing shrug.

Ankh khuli andhe ki, toh vaat lagi dhande ki, thought Virkar. He wondered where to begin, and then decided to go with the hard facts. 'Tracy Barton was murdered by the Smooth Operator.'

His bland statement did not change the set expression on Raashi's face.

'And you've drawn this conclusion from the information Bhoir gave you?' she asked in a flat tone.

'Yes, from what Bhoir told me I can conclude that Akurle and Bhandari didn't do it. Neither did Colasco, because he was in Mumbai at that time. That leaves only the Smooth Operator and the Compass Box Killer. Keeping in mind the Compass Box Killer's revengeful killing of the others, the only person who is left as the prime suspect in Tracy's murder is the Smooth Operator.'

Raashi's eyes registered something that Virkar found difficult to understand as he continued giving her details of the information he had gleaned from Bhoir. 'Tracy was brought in with strangulation marks on her neck. She was apparently strangled by someone with their bare hands after sex.'

Raashi lowered her gaze and looked away, trying hard not to let Virkar read her feelings. However, Virkar was too quick for her. He had already noticed the thin film of moisture that had welled up in the corner of her eyes. He was just a little surprised at her reaction. He had thought that she was hard as nails, but here she was, displaying empathy towards someone she didn't even know. As Raashi's shoulders began to tremble, the confusion that clouded Virkar's mind disappeared. Although he tried to control himself, he couldn't help reaching out with his hand and touching her on the shoulder in an attempt to comfort her. As his fingers touched the bare skin near her collarbone, he felt a tiny spark deep within the synapses of his brain. Raashi turned to look at him. A few teardrops had escaped from her eyes and were running down her cheeks. 'I didn't know...' her voice cracked before the dam broke. Tears began to flow freely and a tortured cry escaped her mouth. Her shoulders began to shudder violently, so much so that Virkar felt the desperate need to hold them tight just to steady them. When her eyes connected with his, she held his gaze for just a few seconds before breaking away...and laying her head against his chest. Surprised, Virkar didn't react but let the warmth of her forehead radiate through the fabric of his T-shirt to his skin.

But when the wetness of her cheeks also permeated to his chest, his arms rose almost of their own accord. Virkar wrapped them around Raashi's back, feeling something electric inside him as he drew her closer to him, engulfing her in the breadth of his chest. Feeling her warm softness against him, Virkar suddenly began to feel helpless against the emotions that were growing within him and dictating his actions. He was still struggling with himself, almost afraid to move, when she raised a soft palm and touched his cheek. Looking down upon her upturned face, he took only a second to read her eyes and, finding an open invitation there, lowered his face and rested his lips on hers. Unsure of how to proceed, Virkar waited. But Raashi had known exactly where this was going. Her tongue darted out from between her parted lips and made its way into Virkar's waiting mouth. He felt her tongue connect with his and let himself be manoeuvred into the kiss...a kiss that went on almost forever. There was a mini explosion in his brain as he felt the sparks down to his toes; his body felt as though it was on fire. Just when he thought that he couldn't take it anymore, he felt Raashi nimble fingers working the buttons of his shirt. As his shirt front fell open to allow her better access, she began to rub her palms gently against the expanse of his chest, making her way down to the waistband of his cargo shorts. Virkar felt the urgent need to reciprocate. He slid his hand to the base of her spine and was about to go further down when she unzipped his cargo shorts and set him free. Virkar couldn't hold himself back anymore.

There, in the cold, damp room in Khandala, Virkar had the hottest sex he had ever had in his life.

29

The killer sat hidden on the thick tree branch listening to the sounds of lovemaking emanating from the window below him.

He had waited until dusk had fallen and, using the cover of darkness, made his way through the thicket of trees outside Katrak Villa towards the only window that was lit up. The thick foliage outside the window had served him well, allowing him to climb up to a vantage point on the tree trunk from which he could see directly into the room. Not satisfied, he had crawled on to a branch that hung above the window till he could hear the voices of Virkar and Raashi inside the room. As luck would have it, he had just been in time to hear Virkar's findings.

He had frozen, his limbs turning to lead. He felt as though a huge crushing weight was squeezing the life out of him. He waited for the feeling to pass, wondering why he felt this way when he had always known that something like what Virkar had described had happened to Tracy.

His mind reeled back nine years to when he had arrived at the Lonavala railway station early one evening. Without wasting any time, he took an autorickshaw to Khandala Police Station. Clutching the small newspaper clipping about Tracy's accident, he made his way to the entrance, only to run directly into the guard.

'Kai paije? What do you want?' the constable on duty said rudely, stopping him. He showed the newspaper clipping to the constable. 'I've come to enquire about this case.' The constable grabbed the clipping from his hand and glanced at it. Then the policeman sneered. 'And how are you concerned with his case? Who are you to the victim?'

'I...I...' he trailed off, trying to find the right words to explain his relationship with Tracy. Finally he chose something that was closest to what he felt. 'I'm her well-wisher.'

The constable dropped his sneer and replaced it with incredulous laughter. 'A well-wisher! You!'

'Yes,' he answered, choosing not to respond to the man's derision.

'Well then, Mr Well-Wisher, what're you doing here? Why aren't you at her funeral?'

'Funeral?' Suddenly, the finality of her death hit him like a hard slap across his cheek. Without wasting any more time, he opened his wallet, took out the hundred-rupee note that was carefully folded inside and handed it to the constable. 'Where?'

On seeing his reaction, the constable suddenly realized that there might actually be some connection between him and Tracy and decided to stop laughing at him. 'The Christian Cemetery,' he said instead, swiftly pocketing the money.

The killer turned and rushed out of the police station compound towards the nearest autorickshaw stand. Waving one down, he promised the driver an extra fifty rupees if he increased his speed. He reached the Christian Cemetery in twenty minutes.

A chowkidar was stamping his feet and warming himself by a small fire beside the iron gates of the cemetery.

This time, the killer was ready. 'I'm Tracy Barton's well-wisher.

Please tell me where the funeral is.' The chowkidar took one look at his dishevelled state and decided he was telling the truth.

The chowkidar pointed at a path that led deep inside the cemetery to where Tracy's grave was being dug. 'Walk down this path for five minutes and you'll come to a marble cross. Take a left from there and walk for a couple of minutes more, you'll find it.'

The killer entered the cemetery and looked down the path that led through the rows of old graves. Dusk had fallen by now. A sudden wind swept past the cemetery unannounced, making the leaves in the trees flutter ominously and he gulped, feeling a sudden chill. As he began to walk down the path, he heard the chowkidar call out from behind him. 'Hurry!'

He whipped around, his heart missing a beat.

The chowkidar called out again. 'Hurry! The coffin might be in the ground already.'

The killer lowered his head against the wind, tightened the strap of his backpack and increased his pace. A few minutes later, he was at the marble cross. He turned left, directly into the path of the blowing wind. In the failing light, he could make out some figures moving in the distance. He quickened his pace, now practically running. As he neared the moving figures, he noticed a thickset man standing in front of two men who were shovelling the last bits of loose earth on a mound in front of a wooden cross. Remembering Tracy's description, he was quite sure that the thickset man was Nigel Colasco.

Colasco took out a mobile phone and dialled a number. He spoke into the phone almost immediately: 'You don't have to worry anymore. It's all taken care of.' The wind blowing towards him carried Colasco's words loud and clear. The killer had been about to call out to them to stop and wait for him, but no words came out of his mouth. But one of the men, sensing an unwanted presence, turned in his direction. Luckily, the killer gathered his wits by then and lay flat on the ground between two graves, his ears straining to hear every word Colasco spoke. As the killer watched, the two men shovelled the last bits of earth on to the mound while keeping a sharp lookout for any intruder.

Colasco handed a wad of notes to the two men and waved them away. The men turned in the direction of the cemetery's gate and receded into the night. Colasco resumed his phone conversation, his voice carrying clearly over the wind to the killer. 'Of course I'm sure! I'm standing over her grave. Bhandari has been paid off, and so has Akurle. I've got all the documents with me. According to them, she died in a car accident, the car that she borrowed for me, and I, as her closest friend and well-wisher, conducted the funeral and laid her to rest.' The killer saw Colasco walk back in the direction of the iron gates while listening to the person on the other end of the phone. 'Yes, may she rest in peace,' Colasco said before hanging up.

The killer had felt a massive urge to run to the freshly dug grave, but he knew that the chowkidar would tell Colasco about his arrival, so he lay there on the grass for a few hours, blending with the earth, lying almost as still as the people lying below the graves. He remained so well hidden that all the attempts of the chowkidar and Colasco—who soon returned to find him— proved unsuccessful. The killer heard their hurried footsteps and snippets of their furtive conversation while he lay pressed to the cold ground. Colasco and the chowkidar continued with their search, wondering where the 'intruder' had vanished. When they finally left, he could only assume that they were looking for him frantically because Colasco was scared that his telephone conversation might have been overheard by him.

After all these years, the killer still remembered how terrified he had been that night. If these ruthless men could have put kind, angelic Tracy into the ground without any compunction, he could only imagine how easy it would have been for them to do the same to him. He had wet himself as that thought crossed his mind. Somewhere in the middle of the night, he had got up from his hiding place, and in the meagre light of the waxing moon, climbed over the cemetery's wall and ran...running until his chest felt as though it would explode. Then he had slowed to a brisk walk, not stopping till he reached a small town somewhere down in the valley.

The sun had risen to reveal that he was in Khopoli. Thereafter, a bus had taken him to Mumbai and a train had taken him back home.

Now, nine years later, he was back, lying as still as a dead man on the branch of a tree while he finally heard another person voice the sordid details of a truth he had always known.

The killer moved back into the dense foliage. Taking care not to make even the slightest sound, he slid to the ground. Slithering into the thicket behind Katrak Villa, he disappeared.

30

Advocate Kirit Shah had his consultation chambers on the third floor of Taiyabji Terrace, a small building on Rope Walk Lane, off Rampart Row, Kala Ghoda. From his chambers he found it extremely convenient to access the High Court of Bombay, where he pleaded cases for his corporate clients. For many years, he had maintained a routine of leaving the High Court sharp at the 5.00 p.m. closing time and walking back to his chambers to begin conducting client meetings from 5.15 p.m. onwards.

As was his habit, he was climbing up the stairs of Taiyabji Terrace at 5.12 p.m. when he was accosted by a young man, who, from his appearance, looked like some kind of a legal professional.

He smiled at Shah. 'Hello, sir, I'm Anay Vansode. I was your student five years ago when you used to lecture at the Government Law College. Don't you remember me?'

'Ah, yes...I remember,' lied Shah, not wanting to show that he had no memory of the young man. He was bad with faces and names. In any case, this was a usual occurrence; people who had been his students at some time or the other were constantly stopping him in the vicinity of the High Court.

'Come walk with me and tell me what it is that you want,' said the advocate, not wanting to waste precious minutes. The rich litigants waiting for him in his chambers were his priority.

'Sir, I have a small NGO called Jhopadpatti Children Sudhaar Sanstha; we partner up with Slum Baalak Suraksha for many schemes.'

Advocate Shah stopped. 'Ah, okay, you work with Nigel's NGO. He was my close friend.'

'Yes, sir, I believe so,' replied the man.

'Poor Nigel. What a way to go!' said the advocate, shaking his head.

'Sir, he is gone, but his going has created a financial crunch for us. We were dependent on him for financial aid. Now we need to find some funds quickly if we are to carry on our work.'

Shah frowned. 'What's that got to do with me?'

'Well, you're the person who manages all the legal affairs for Slum Baalak Suraksha, aren't you?'

The advocate looked wary. 'Yes, yes...but just come to the point. I've got people waiting for me. What is it that you want?'

'To cut a long story short, can you please arrange a meeting with the financial contributors who finance Slum Baalak Suraksha? I can plead our case independently.'

Advocate Shah had by now reached the door to his chambers. He turned and looked the young man straight in the face. He held his gaze for a long moment. 'Vansode, is it?' he asked finally.

The young man nodded.

Advocate Shah took out a crisp visiting card and handed it to the young man. 'Give me a call after a couple of days. I'll try to fix up some meetings for next week. I have people waiting for me now. Please excuse me,' he nodded and swiftly walked through the door.

As soon as the door shut behind him, Shah dashed through his crowded waiting room, paying no heed to the anxious faces that looked up at him. He ran into his office and all the way to his private chamber. Shutting and locking the door behind him, he sat down. He pulled out his mobile phone and dialled a number. After three rings, the phone was picked up on the other side.

'Crime Branch headquarters,' a voice said.

'I want to speak to the person in charge of the Compass Box Killer case… Inspector Virkar, isn't it?'

'Sir, Inspector Virkar is not—'

'Please connect me to Inspector Virkar. I want to speak to him immediately. It's a matter of life and death,' shouted Advocate Shah into the phone, his brow moist with sweat.

'Please hold on,' said the man on the other end.

A couple of excruciating minutes later, a deep, throaty voice said, 'Inspector Virkar here.'

'Inspector, I've just met the Compass Box Killer.'

Virkar had returned that morning from Khandala after having spent the previous night holed up in the room at Katrak Villa with Raashi. They had discussed the case threadbare between unending bouts of lovemaking. They would still be there had it not been for the fact that, early in the morning, he had received a text from ACP Wagh asking him to report back to the Crime Branch for filing the paperwork required to fully handover the case. He had been toiling through the case papers when the constable on duty had summoned him to answer Advocate Shah's call.

Now, seated in the soft, cushioned leather seat normally reserved for the well-heeled clientele that visited Advocate Shah,

Virkar looked into the eyes of the lawyer who was still trembling with fear.

'But how can you be so sure that it was him?' asked Virkar.

'Please, Inspector. I've been a lawyer for over twenty-five years and those years haven't been spent in vain.'

But Virkar persisted. 'Are you sure it was him?'

Shah explained, 'I can say it with full surety. Although, I don't practice criminal law, I follow criminal cases very closely, and this case is of my friend Nigel's murder. Of *course* I remember the police sketch of the alleged killer.'

Virkar rubbed his jaw. 'But why would he come to you asking to arrange meetings for him?'

'To get me to some secure location and kill me, of course!'

Virkar raised his hand. 'Relax, sir. If he wanted to kill you, you would be dead already. He obviously just wanted the information that he asked for.'

'I'm just Nigel's friend and a legal advisor to his NGO. Sometimes I help draw up papers to help foreigners and NRIs adopt slum children. But I do all this pro bono—free of cost. I'm not involved in raising funds or dealing with the contributors themselves.'

'Hmm…you knew Nigel Colasco for a long time?' said Virkar, rubbing his chin.

'Well…yes. He was my classmate at the Government Law College but I lost touch with him after we graduated. Later, when my wife and I learnt we could not have children, I reconnected with Nigel. I'd heard about the work he was doing and thought he could help us.' The advocate paused and stared into the distance. 'He helped us adopt a beautiful baby boy. Nigel was a rakhi-brother to my wife and the godfather of my ward.'

Virkar found something odd in what the lawyer had just said.

But before he could gather his thoughts, the door to the chamber swung open and his colleague, Senior Inspector Sonavane, and two sub-inspectors entered.

'Advocate Kirit Shah, I'm the Inspector in charge of the Compass Box Killer case.'

Virkar got up at once. Facing Sonavane, he shrugged. 'The advocate asked for me by name. He seemed very disturbed. So I came here.'

'Thank you, Virkar. You can leave now,' Sonavane shot back.

Virkar nodded at Advocate Shah and left the room.

But as he stepped outside, his pulse started racing. There was a word the advocate had used that rang alarm bells in his head. Ward. Suddenly, another piece of the puzzle had clicked into place, like the bolt of a well-oiled gun. Shah had used the legal word for his adopted child—'ward'. *Of course! Colasco had used legalese too!* Virkar realized. Colasco was a lawyer by profession and was probably prone to using legal terminology. Lawyers tend to use the archaic English terms that they use at work in their daily lives, too, at times. Colasco did so even when he was dying. Virkar cursed himself for not thinking of it before. He narrowed his eyes as Colasco's dying words replayed in his mind. 'Hurry… Tracy's ward'. Colasco hadn't been referring to a *hospital* ward; instead, he had been talking about a child under the supervision of a guardian—in this case, under Tracy's. Since she worked only with orphans, 'Tracy's ward' most probably meant that Colasco was referring to an orphan who had been adopted by Tracy.

A little orphan who had grown to become a killer.

31

By late evening, the garden behind the C.G.S. Colony on Antop Hill was full of people out for an evening stroll. A group of motivated women from a local resident association had converted the plot earlier used as a garbage dump into the flourishing green oasis that it now was. This shining example of citizens' initiative was triggered the morning people living in the buildings around had found a fresh corpse lying in the garbage. Hence, the women of the society had taken it upon themselves to turn the dump that was a refuge for drug addicts into a middle-class haven.

As Virkar strolled along the walking track in the garden while trying not to upset the rhythm of the strolling residents, his eyes searched through the dying light, trying to catch sight of Lourdes D'Monte. The children playing outside Lourdes' C.G.S. colony building had told him that Lourdes aunty was out for her evening walk around this garden. Suddenly, Virkar saw her walking purposefully a few steps ahead of him, ridiculously attired in a polyester skirt-blouse and sports shoes. Deep in conversation with another woman wearing similar clothes, she was huffing and puffing along the circuitous walking path, trying hard to melt the kilos that had crept up on her over the years. Virkar didn't want to surprise her, so he increased his speed and walked past her. Reaching a bench that lay ahead, he sat down, waiting for her to notice him as she came up the path. Lourdes saw Virkar when she was still about fifteen steps away from him. A look of discomfort crossed her face as she recognized him as the same policeman who had knocked on her door at an early morning hour not so long ago. But it disappeared as soon as Virkar flashed her a friendly smile. He rose from his seat and greeted her politely. In turn, she stopped and stood next to him, asking her friend to carry on.

As soon as Lourdes' friend was out of earshot, Virkar spoke. 'I'm sorry for having come unannounced, but I couldn't get through to your mobile phone.'

An expressionless Lourdes replied, 'I suppose I must at least thank you for coming at a decent hour, Inspector Virkar.'

Virkar smiled sheepishly and ran his fingers through his hair.

Loudres continued, 'I keep my phone switched off on Sundays so that I'm not disturbed by unnecessary people. Besides, I go to church for service.'

'I'd like to ask you a few questions,' Virkar ventured.

Lourdes' face hardened. 'I've spoken to our Parish priest and he's promised to take me to the Archbishop if I'm troubled by the police.'

Virkar realized that it was not going to be easy this time. 'Look, I just need your help to find Tracy's killer. I've been to her grave, may God rest her soul in peace.'

Lourdes solemnly drew the sign of the cross against her body, but her voice was icy. 'As I understand from the newspapers, you are off the case, Inspector.'

'I don't have to be on the case to find justice for the innocent,' said Virkar without batting an eyelid. Lourdes' expression softened. This was the opening Virkar needed. He got straight to the point. 'What I'd like to know is, did Tracy ever tell you that she had adopted a child?'

Lourdes's mouth set in a firm line. 'Inspector, Tracy was not my close friend. She didn't share any intimate details of her life with me.'

Virkar, however, refused to back down. 'But maybe she gave you an impression that she had a special bond with a particular child among those under the care of the Slum Baalak Suraksha. An orphan boy, perhaps?'

'Inspector, most of our children are orphans. Tracy was in contact with so many of them. She loved them all,' said Lourdes wearily.

'I agree. But what I'm trying to get at, Lourdes, is whether Tracy was emotionally attached to any particular boy from among the many she cared for.'

Lourdes fell silent for a moment. Virkar watched her face, hopeful. Then she shook her head. 'No. No particular boy comes to my mind.'

Virkar was starting to feel desperate now. 'In our first meeting, you told me that she had been supporting orphans even while she was a student in the UK? Do you know which organizations she sent the money to from the UK?'

Lourdes smiled indulgently at Virkar. 'To ours, for one. That's how we got acquainted.'

'Hmm...where else do you think she would have sent money? Perhaps some other kind of charitable organization... an orphanage, for instance?'

Lourdes lapsed into thoughtful silence.

'Well, now that you ask me, Inspector, Tracy used to make a lot of trips to different parts of the country visiting NGOs, old people's homes, orphanages and such. Once, I remember seeing some letters she had left behind in our office by mistake; they were from some orphanage out of town. I don't remember too clearly now…it was a long time ago.'

'Do you remember anything at all about the orphanage?' Virkar asked hopefully.

Lourdes shook her head. 'No, sorry. It happened years ago.'

Virkar's shoulders drooped. 'Well, thank you for trying. If you recollect anything at all, please call me. You have my number.'

Lourdes nodded. Virkar turned and started walking back to his Bullet, debating whether he should go to Slum Baalak Suraksha's office and speak to the garrulous watchman who had been with the NGO ever since its inception. But he realized that it was a long shot.

Virkar felt frustrated. He was clutching at straws in his attempt to crack this case.

'Inspector Virkar…' a voice called out from behind. He turned to see Lourdes hurrying down the walking track towards him.

'I just remembered something,' she said, a little breathlessly. Virkar felt a renewed surge of hope.

'Once, when she came back from a trip out of town, she looked very despondent. When I asked her what was wrong, she didn't tell me much except that she was missing some special person. I remember thinking at first that it was a lover, but later I felt that it was a child she was talking about.'

'How can you say this for sure? Did she confide in you later?' Virkar asked.

Lourdes shook her head and shrugged. 'No, it was just… maybe just a mother's instinct.'

'Hmm…do you remember where Tracy had returned from?' Virkar asked.

'From Belgaum,' she replied without hesitation, her crinkly eyes shining at the memory. 'I remember because she had made a joke about it, saying that she had returned from "Belgium", and we had laughed about it.'

Virkar's heart skipped a beat as he realized that he had just unearthed a very important clue. The Compass Box Killer had been identified as a man, someone who spoke fluent Marathi and Kannada, perhaps hailing from the Maharashtra-Karnataka border.

Somebody from a place like...Belgaum.

32

Belgaum

Hotel Akshata is famous across North Karnataka for its fresh seafood and for the warm hospitality experienced by all those who choose to spend a few nights in the hotel's simple but comfortable rooms. Located in the Bogarves area in the heart of Belgaum, its majestic frontage blends in among what is left of the old houses of the Bogars or coppersmiths who used to live in that area.

Virkar checked into the hotel along with Raashi at 4.00 p.m. in the afternoon. They had left Mumbai at 6.00 a.m. that morning, breaking only for a quick bite at a highway dhaba on NH 4. The night before, Virkar had landed up at Raashi's Andheri flat after having told her that he needed to meet her urgently. Virkar was not sure where his relationship with her was headed, but he had grown to respect and like her. He especially appreciated her logical, quick-thinking mind. As soon as he reached her flat, he had begun to babble about his discovery that the Compass Box Killer could be connected to Belgaum. But Raashi had placed a finger on his lips and dragged him into the shower where she had proceeded to wash the tiredness out of his body. He had wanted to talk afterwards but she had led him to bed for a passionate bout of lovemaking. Even when they lay satiated in each other's arms, Virkar had tried to open the topic for discussion, only to be shushed again. They could get into details on their way to Belgaum the next morning, he was told. Virkar had smiled and immediately fallen asleep then, only to rise the next morning at 5.00 a.m. when he felt Raashi's gentle touch on his face. He had quickly showered and they had left together on his Bullet, stopping only to pick up some fresh clothes and his backpack from his Bhoiwada quarters.

It was close to 4.00 p.m. when they reached Belgaum, and the first thing they did after checking into Hotel Akshata was to ask for directions to the office of the Belgaum city corporation. Making their way to the corporation office, located nearby, they managed to get a list of orphanages from a clerk who was ready to help as soon as Raashi flashed a winsome smile and a hundred-rupee note at him. As Belgaum was a small border town, the list was not a long one. Virkar picked out the two Christian orphanages as their first points of call. One was the Priory Children's Home that was located on the outskirts of the Belgaum-Panjim National Highway and would take them a couple of hours to reach. Virkar and Raashi decided to head there the next morning since it was already past working hours, opting instead to visit the other Christian orphanage on the list which was located in the nearby cantonment area of Belgaum.

The Belgaum cantonment area, normally referred to as the 'Camp' area, was built by the British during their rule in India. Apart from military buildings, its cool and green environs display a number of well-preserved colonial buildings that house schools, churches and an orphanage. As Virkar and Raashi rode the Bullet through its tree-lined lanes, they felt transported back in time. As they parked the Bullet and walked through the arched gate of St. Francis D'Assisi Orphanage and School, the excited cries of little children getting ready for their evening meal filled the air. In the fading light, Virkar and Raashi could still make out the magnificent gothic building that housed the orphanage, built entirely in Gokak pink stone. When they asked to see the person in charge of the orphanage, a young assistant ushered them into Reverend Anthony's office.

Reverend Anthony, a tall, thickly bespectacled man with a goatee and the air of an erstwhile athelete, had just returned from daily mass and was getting ready for his evening meal. But on seeing that his visitors had come all the way from Mumbai, he decided to give them a few minutes. Virkar and Raashi introduced themselves as they took their seats.

Virkar decided to adopt a deferential tone when he said, 'We don't want to take up too much of your time, Reverend, but we wanted to ask if you happened to know a British lady called Tracy Barton?'

The Reverend's benevolent expression did not change as he looked at Virkar and Raashi closely.

Finally, he asked, 'And how are you connected to her?'

'We're not. Actually, we're looking for a person from your orphanage who might have been here a few years ago...someone who may have been her ward.'

'What is all this about, though?' asked the Reverend.

'Well, it's a long, complicated story. But we feel that this person might be involved in some criminal activity.'

The Reverend looked at his watch and then at them. 'Sorry, I don't know of any such boy. Now, if you will excuse me, I have urgent work to take care of.'

'But *do* you know Tracy Barton, Reverend?' Raashi butted in.

The Reverend shook his head. 'We're not allowed to give out any information about the children's guardians to anyone.'

'So does that mean you did know Tracy? Was she a guardian of someone here?' Raashi flashed him a winning smile.

The Reverend returned an even broader smile as he replied, 'My dear girl, I must say that your smile is rather nice. But its charms will not work on me. I'm a priest, you see.' He walked to the open door of his office and stood there, indicating that he would like his visitors to leave.

Raashi was reluctant but Virkar caught her elbow and gently guided her out. Once under the arched gate outside, he said, 'There was no need to put the Reverend in a spot. It was clear that he was lying. Didn't you notice that he referred to the ward as a "boy"? I didn't mention the ward's gender.'

Raashi gave him a hurt look that he ignored. He looked around in the dark, trying to spot something.

'So, Mr Smart Inspector, what are we going to do now?' Raashi asked.

'We are going to go back to the hotel and have an early dinner.'

'And then?'

'And then I'll come back here and go through the records in their office.'

Raashi looked a little unsure. 'Will you be able to get inside?'

'Of course! His door has the old British style locks. No problem.'

Raashi made a mock grimace. 'Virkar, sometimes I wonder whether you're a policeman or a thief.'

'I'm a bit of both,' he smiled as he straddled his Bullet.

Raashi hugged him tight as she sat behind him.

'By the way, did you see any dogs lurking around while we were inside the orphanage?' enquired Virkar.

'No, there were no dogs. Why?' she asked, puzzled.

'Because I don't want to be bitten when I come here later tonight.'

33

But Raashi was wrong. Virkar cursed under his breath, wishing he had gone with his instincts and checked instead of taking Raashi's word for it. The dogs in the orphanage were not merely guard dogs—they were highly trained attack dogs. Why an orphanage in Belgaum needed attack dogs to defend it was a question that Virkar had no answer for. Not that he had time to stand around and mull over this; he was too busy running for his life. The attack dogs, obviously trained to bark only to signal their mates, had waited until Virkar was well inside the orphanage's premises before cornering him. Whipping around at the first half-bark, Virkar had realized that his way back to the wall that he had jumped over had been cut off by two rapidly advancing Doberman Pinschers. Virkar quickly surmised that the only shelter he had was the orphanage building itself. He decided to run to the part of the building that was closest to him: the office block. As luck would have it, the door to the office block was not locked. Obviously the keepers of the orphanage were quite confident of the efficacy of their attack dogs. Thanking his stars that he didn't have to clamber up a pipe, Virkar rushed in through the door and slammed it behind him with only seconds to spare. As he stood inside panting in relief, he heard the muted grunts of the two Dobermans as their bodies slammed against the old wood of the door. Before he could fully catch his breath, the light bulb above him was switched on with an unceremonious click. Behind him, a voice said, 'You were lucky. They're trained to tear a man's arm off his body.'

Suddenly, the dogs began to bark loudly. Virkar turned around to see Reverend Anthony standing at the head of the staircase behind him, dressed in pajamas and a maroon, silk housecoat. Virkar wondered whether Reverend Anthony had any other tricks up his sleeve apart from flesh-tearing attack dogs. He eyed the priest's hands that were clenched inside the pockets of the housecoat. There seemed to be something in there along with the Reverend's clenched fist, something that Virkar was familiar with and didn't particularly like. As if reading his mind, Reverend Anthony took his right hand out from the pocket, confirming Virkar's fears—his fist was wrapped around a small, antique revolver that had been famous at the turn of the century: a Webley make known as the British Bulldog. As the Reverend levelled the gun towards him, Virkar didn't really feel like taking a chance on finding out whether it still worked. Realizing that there was no other way out, he decided to come to the point. 'He's going to die if you don't tell me who he is.'

Father Anthony seemed to consider his words while his finger absentmindedly stroked the trigger.

'Something bad happened to Tracy Barton and I believe he's taking revenge for it. But they'll kill him if I don't get to him first.'

The barking of the dogs now rose sharply behind him and suddenly Father Anthony yelled out loud: 'Laurel, Hardy, quiet!' Immediately, the dogs fell silent, much like a switch had been flipped. The tension in Reverend Anthony's fist eased as he lowered the gun. Virkar watched him warily as he walked down the stairs towards him. The Reverend reached out for him and, holding Virkar's hand in his, said, 'Son, he's misguided. All he wants is love. Please save him.'

Virkar nodded. Reverend Anthony turned and led him towards his office. Once inside, he walked behind his desk and sat down on his chair. He motioned Virkar towards the chair across the table. After Virkar was seated, Reverend Anthony began: 'About sixteen years ago, a British aid organization, Arms Around Orphans, contacted us with a unique plan. They would find sponsors in the UK for each orphan that we had here. Each child would be sponsored with school materials, clothes and fees for boarding and lodging. It was through this programme that a fifteen-year-old girl from the UK began to send us money to sponsor a ten-year-old boy. She used to save up her pocket money every month to be able to send us the fifty pounds we required for the sponsorship. Part of the programme was to let there be written and telephonic communication between the sponsor and the child. In this particular case, the relationship between Tracy and the boy grew stronger because Tracy was an orphan as well. The boy flowered into a student with superior intelligence and passed out from here with flying colours. But somehow he couldn't make it through competitive entrance tests, so Tracy, who by then had saved up enough money from her well-paying job, sponsored him into an engineering college. The boy was one of the best students of the college till the day Tracy died. It all went downhill from there.' Reverend Anthony lapsed into a meditative silence.

Virkar waited for him to begin again, but the priest was lost in his thoughts. It was only when Virkar saw that tears had began to streak down the Reverend's cheeks that he asked softly, 'What happened then, Reverend?'

'The boy came to me one day and told me that he suspected

Tracy had been murdered. He had been to Khandala and had returned with this theory. But I thought that he was just emotionally disturbed and brushed his theory aside.'

'Did he say anything about somebody called the Smooth Operator?'

'I don't remember,' said the priest. 'He said a lot of things, and it all seemed so ridiculous that I was upset with him.'

'What did you do?'

'I called up the director of the engineering college and told him to give the boy a few days off as he was emotionally disturbed.'

'And did they?'

Reverend Anthony sat back in his seat; his body seemed to have shrunk in size in the past few minutes. Finally, he sighed and said, 'No. Instead, they threw him out of the college. You see, there was no one left to pay his fees.'

Virkar gave him a stern stare. 'But, surely *you* could have paid his fees, Reverend?' The Reverend shrank further into his seat but this time he was squirming with discomfort. Somewhat defensively, he said, 'I have two hundred children who I look after...everything that I earn goes into the orphanage. I don't have a single paisa in my name.'

Virkar continued to stare at him; slowly, a sense of understanding replaced the indignation he felt. 'What happened then?' he asked, his tone gentler this time.

Suddenly Reverend Anthony looked very tired. 'It's a long story, son, but it concludes with the boy ending up in jail.'

34

'Hari Prasad...his name is Hari Prasad.' Virkar saw the shock of realization in Raashi's eyes as soon as he said this.

'Yes, I've realized it too,' he said before Raashi could say anything.

The dying Colasco had, in fact, told them everything. He had said, 'Hari...Tracy's ward' and not 'Hurry...Tracy's ward'.

Virkar had spent the entire night riding around the dark streets of Belgaum on his Bullet after leaving the orphanage. In his head, he kept going over the sequence of events. *Colasco knew Hari's identity and his relationship with Tracy, and perhaps also knew that Hari was Akurle and Bhandari's killer. But something had stopped Colasco from sharing this crucial information with the police. Was it the fear of revealing the crime that he himself had committed? Or was it the fear of someone else—the Smooth Operator, perhaps?*

By the time Virkar made his way back to the hotel, it was dawn and Raashi had fallen asleep waiting for him to return.

Over breakfast, Virkar told Raashi what Reverend Anthony had told him, and more. Hari was not granted admission into his final year even though he was a brilliant student and had been topping his class every year. To earn money to pay his fees and gain re-entry into the final year, Hari had started teaching at a local coaching class. But as he hadn't been able to cope with Tracy's death, he became depressed and started having mood swings. In one such disturbed moment, he had fought with the owner of the coaching class over some underhand deductions in his salary. Hari lost his temper and beat the owner, destroying some coaching class property in the process. Instead of being treated for depression caused due to his circumstances, Hari had been convicted on drummed up charges of 'attempted murder' and imprisoned at the Central Prison at Barudanga.

Considered the equivalent of Andaman's infamous Kala Pani jail, the Central Prison at Barudanga, spread over an area of about 150 acres, was built by the British in the 1920s. The dreaded jail has two hexagonal sections. The first hexagon comprises of barracks where the convicted prisoners, both short-term and those convicted for life, are made to stay and work. The second hexagon has blocks where those prisoners who are under trial are lodged. The prison has the facility to hang people and has three gallows. And, therefore, all prisoners sentenced to capital punishment are lodged in Barudanga. Among sundry criminals like murders and rapists, it also houses SIMI terrorists, members of the dreaded Dandupalya gang and members of Veerappan's forest-poaching gang.

The prison was only about fifteen kilometres away from the main Belgaum city, a distance that Virkar covered in about twenty minutes. But not before Raashi spent two hours making phone calls to secure the required permission to visit the prison. She had finally swung it by calling in a favour from a contact in the Information and Broadcasting Ministry in Delhi who telephoned someone in the Secretariat at Bangalore, who, in turn, telephoned the Director of Prisons with a request to grant them permission to meet with the superintendent of Barudanga Prison.

The superintendent, V. K. Joseph, was cordial towards them even though they had barged in unceremoniously. But as soon as they were seated in front of the superintendent, Virkar decided to dispense with all niceties and came straight to the point. 'Joseph saheb, we want to know everything about a prisoner who was jailed here—Hari Prasad.'

The superintendent looked thoughtful. 'Hmm…Hari Prasad. I don't seem to remember him…let me see.' Virkar noticed the defocused and fixated position of superintendent's pupils, indicating that he was lying. The superintendent then motioned to his assistant to bring out the file on the prisoner in question. After sifting through a few pages in the file he said, 'Yes, I remember him now. He was a model prisoner. He was a good influence on a lot of other prisoners, too, especially his cellmate, whom he diligently tutored to secure a BSc degree.'

'I see. And what was he convicted for?' Virkar pressed further.

'For attempted murder and destroying private property. He spent eight years here.'

'Eight years for attempted murder! Isn't that a little too harsh?' asked Virkar.

'Yes, I thought so too, but I am not the judge who sentenced him.'

'When was he released?'

'Uh…about a year ago.'

'About a year ago?' muttered Virkar, as though speaking to himself, and then added, 'Wasn't there some controversial incident here around that time?'

He noticed that the wary look on the superintendent's face now showed hints of fear. Virkar knew that he had suddenly become suspicious that this meeting could be a sting operation or a spot raid. He realized that he needed to do something quickly before the superintendent called the meeting to an end. He darted a look towards Raashi who, as usual, was quick to catch on.

Flashing her broad, disarming smile, she raised her empty palms and showed them to the superintendent for his scrutiny, 'Look, superintendent saheb, we don't have any cameras or any other agenda. This is personal, not official.'

The superintendent seemed to relax a little. 'I was not involved in what happened,' he said. Virkar opened his mouth to ask another question but Raashi squeezed his knee under table. She did not break eye contact with the superintendent, nor did she drop her broad smile. Instead, she infused a tone of compassion into her voice. 'We know,' she said. 'Your record is absolutely clean. We're not here to tarnish your reputation. Just tell us all about Hari Prasad and we'll be on our way.'

The superintendent relaxed further. 'All I can say is that he did us all a favour.'

'Us?' Raashi's question was gentle.

'Well, yes. I mean the prison guards, the prisoners and even the people at large.'

Virkar, who by now was feeling thoroughly confused and impatient, asked, 'What kind of favour?' Unfortunately, Virkar's intervention broke the spell that Raashi had cast over the superintendent. He blinked, realizing that he had been led into sharing more than he should have. He clamped up, turning his attention to some papers on his desk and pretending to busy himself in them. Virkar looked all set to launch into an interrogation but Raashi squeezed his knee once again, calming him down.

'Sir,' Raashi addressed the superintendent, 'I understand that you may not want to share the details yourself, but maybe you can tell us how we can get this information ourselves?'

The superintendent sat still, looking thoughtful. He seemed to be considering Raashi's statement. But then he rose and said, 'I have to go on my rounds. Please excuse me.'

Raashi, in a frustrated, last-ditch effort, said, 'Superintendent, can you please give us a photograph of Hari from your records?'

'Sure,' said the superintendent, 'as soon as you apply through the proper channels.' He turned and walked out of the room, leaving Virkar and Raashi staring at his receding back.

A few seconds later, the assistant superintendent walked into the room and announced that their meeting was over. Raashi and Virkar rose and followed him out without a word. But just before they could exit the formidable prison gate, Virkar excused himself to go to the bathroom. The assistant superintendent didn't want to take any chances, so he had Virkar escorted by a guard all the way into the visitor's toilets. Raashi was left standing alone near the prison office—a situation that she didn't appreciate at all, for she suddenly became the cynosure of every passing eye. As long as Virkar was with her, nobody had dared to make eye contact, but as soon as she was alone, it was open season. Just when she was thinking that the intensity of everyone's gaze would melt the clothes off her body, Virkar returned, looking nonchalant.

Raashi flung him a dirty look, and, without a word, flounced out of the prison, walking two steps ahead of him till they reached the Bullet parked in the visitor's parking lot. When Virkar geared the Bullet on to the highway, Raashi, who was clinging to him on the back seat, exploding sarcastically into his ear, said, 'Where to now, O mighty Lord Virkar?'

'To Khade Bazaar in Belgaum,' said Virkar matter-of-factly. Raashi was a little taken aback at his response.

'Why?'

'Rahmat Ali Peerzada, Hari's ex-cellmate, the one who Hari tutored for his BSc degree, runs a small computer coaching class there.'

'And how did you find that out?'

'Through improper channels,' Virkar laughed.

Behind him Raashi rolled her eyes in exasperation.

Virkar took his time laughing, and then finally said, 'I bribed the guard who accompanied me to the prison toilet.'

35

When they neared the city, they decided to split up. Virkar had realized that Khade Bazaar was an area where Raashi's presence would work as a disadvantage. And, in any case, they needed to speak to the authorities at Hari Prasad's engineering college to try and get a photograph from their records. Even though it may be a few years old, it was still something that they could work with. Virkar convinced Raashi that they would get results faster if they both pursued their leads individually. After dropping Raashi at the gates of the SUMYCO Institute of Technology, Virkar headed towards the crowded lanes of Khade Bazaar.

Khade Bazaar is one of the central shopping areas of Belgaum, something of a combination of Mumbai's Mohammed Ali Road and Bhuleshwar. Its crowded lanes truly represent a mix of the Marathi-Kannada, Hindu-Muslim culture of Belgaum. The small shops that line the road are tightly bunched together and are always packed with people buying clothes, dry fruits and other household items. Virkar's Bullet made its way slowly through the main road jammed with traffic. His eyes scanned the shopfronts for anything that indicated a computer coaching class. He had to make two passes up and down the road to finally spot the small sign for Bright Computer Education Classes. He had missed it before because it was dangling above a small shopfront between a readymade garment showroom and a pathology lab. Virkar looked for a place to park the Bullet. Not having found one close to his destination, he rode on and located a spot about 500 yards ahead.

But just as he was parking his Bullet, he saw a police jeep pass by him. He turned towards the Bright Computer Education Classes and saw the jeep stop right in front of his destination. Virkar turned his attention towards the window of a readymade garment shop that was now parallel to him. Keeping one eye focused on the entrance of the computer classes, he pretended to be very interested in the children's clothes displayed in front of him. Suddenly, he saw two constables and a sub-inspector emerge from inside Bright Computer Education Classes; they were dragging a slim, middle-aged man along with them. The thick beard on the man's face obscured almost all his features other than his sharp nose. The constables pushed the bearded man into the back of the jeep while the sub-inspector sat in the passenger seat. The jeep took off with a screech, blocking traffic. As it made a sharp U-turn, it roared past Virkar. The small crowd that had gathered to watch the show began to disperse.

Virkar stood still for a minute, trying to figure out his next course of action. Suddenly, he overheard a man who had emerged from the readymade garment shop say to a similarly bearded man behind the counter inside, 'Poor Rahmat Ali...it's difficult to lead an honest life after having been a criminal.' The shopkeeper inside tut-tutted and went back to sorting clothes.

Virkar casually asked the man outside, 'Where have they taken him?'

'Where else?' said the man. 'To the local police station.'

Virkar walked back to the Bullet and made his way to the

local police station after seeking directions. Once outside the station, he lingered, wondering whether to go inside and ask to meet Rahmat Ali Peerzada. But something inside him told him that his visit to the prison that morning and the fact that the police had picked up Rahmat Ali were linked. He decided to wait at a safe distance outside and observe the goings-on.

Afternoon turned to evening after a couple of hours and Virkar soon grew tired of staring at the entrance of the police station. As it began to grow dark, Virkar decided to go inside and ask to see Rahmat Ali after all. Suddenly, he saw Rahmat Ali emerge from within the gates with the look of a freshly beaten-up police detainee. He stood at the entrance and looked around as if trying to spot an empty autorickshaw. Virkar quickly gunned the Bullet and rode it towards him. But as he neared the compound of the police station, he saw another motorcycle ride out of a bylane and begin cruising towards Rahmat Ali from the opposite direction. The two men seated on the motorcycle were staring purposefully at Rahmat Ali. Virkar's trained eye picked up on a sudden movement made by the man on the back seat; he saw that the man had his hand covered with a handkerchief. The way the man was holding his hand left no doubt in Virkar's mind that he had a gun under the cloth.

Virkar glanced at Rahmat Ali who had no idea that he was in danger. Instinctively, Virkar swung his Bullet into the path of the other motorcycle. With the assured action of a man who knows his motorcycles, he jumped off the still moving Bullet just in time, letting it skid in the direction of the two men. By the time the two men became aware of the careening Bullet, it was too late. The Bullet smashed into their legs, throwing them forward as it continued skidding along the road, taking their motorcycle along with it. The two men flew into the air and the rider landed face-first on the bonnet of a passing car. Rolling on to the ground, he lay still. The man with the gun wasn't that lucky; he, too, bounced off the car front but fell directly in the car's path. A loud crunch was heard as his body came under the car. The gun in his hand skidded on the road, spinning and coming to rest in front of the shocked Rahmat Ali who stood rooted to his spot. The loud crash of the Bullet and the other motorcycle coming to a stop against a wall jolted him back to his senses. Virkar, by this time, had steadied himself and was walking towards Rahmat Ali.

Rahmat Ali took one look at the two crushed men and then at Virkar. Deciding not to linger around any longer, he turned and ran as if his life depended on it, which it probably did. Virkar made a move towards Rahmat Ali but was brought to a stop by the shrill whistle of a policeman who had emerged from within the police station. Realizing that the situation might soon get out of hand, Virkar instead ran towards his Bullet. In the confusion created by the crowd surrounding the two men, everyone had forgotten about the motorcycles. Virkar picked up the Bullet and saw that, apart from the scraped paint, the bike was fine. Lifting it off the ground, he rolled it into a bylane, quickly gunning it to a start and made his way away from the scene.

36

'What the hell happened to you, Virkar?' asked a shocked Raashi as he entered the hotel room. Virkar caught his reflection in the almirah's mirror and, for the first time that day, became aware of his dishevelled state. Night had fallen since Virkar's departure from the Khade Bazaar area. He had turned the Bullet on to the highway and ridden out about thirty kilometres towards Goa. He had noted a busy highway hotel specializing in Goan food on the way, so, a couple of kilometres ahead, he had found an abandoned shed and hidden his Bullet inside and proceeded to walk back along the highway towards the restaurant. At the highway restaurant, he had hopped on to a passing State Transport bus and made his way back to Belgaum city. Alighting at the main bus depot, he had caught an autorickshaw to Sambhaji Chowk in Bogarves. Stopping the autorickshaw about half a kilometre from the hotel, he had completed the rest of his journey on foot. Standing outside the hotel for about fifteen minutes, he had observed every passerby until he was sure that no one was waiting for him. Then he had made his way back up to the hotel room, only to be greeted by a worried Raashi.

'I don't have time to explain; we have to get out of here now,' said Virkar. As quickly as he could, he began to gather his things and shoving them into his backpack.

Raashi was a little slow to respond. 'But…what happened?' she asked again.

'I'll tell you when we're safely out of here. Get your things together.'

Something in Virkar's tone snapped her out of her daze. She, too, began to quickly stuff her things into her bag. But just as they were ready to leave, there was a knock on the door. Virkar froze. He raised his finger to his lips, motioning Raashi to be quiet. Then he removed the bed lamp from its socket and stood behind the door, poised to strike anyone who may come through it. He signalled Raashi to open the door.

Raashi walked up to the door and opened it only a crack. Peeping through it, she asked, 'Yes? What is it?'

'The man on the Bullet… I want to talk to him,' said a shaky voice from the other side of the door.

'Who are you?' she enquired.

'Rahmat Ali Peerzada.'

Raashi shut the door without saying anything. Virkar quickly exchanged positions with her, handing her the lamp and motioning her to strike if anything seemed untoward. Then he opened the door, but again only just a crack. Virkar saw the bearded man whose life he had saved earlier that evening.

Rahmat Ali Peerzada looked at him and said, 'I've come to thank you and to tell you whatever you want to know about Hari Prasad.'

Virkar shot back, 'How do you know what I want?'

'The prison network works outside the prison, too, saheb. My network was a little slow today, but thanks to you, I'm unharmed.'

Virkar opened the door just enough to pop his head out and

look up and down the corridor to see if Rahmat Ali Peerzada had any friends lurking in the shadows. Satisfied that the man was alone, Virkar opened the door and let him in. But as soon as he was in the room, Virkar pushed him against the wall and carefully searched his body for any concealed weapons. Rahmat Ali stood silently while Virkar conducted his search.

When Virkar was absolutely sure that Rahmat Ali was unarmed, he relaxed. In a brusque tone, he asked, 'Why did they want to kill you?'

Rahmat Ali's eyes were expressionless. 'To answer that, I have to start from the very beginning.'

When Virkar nodded, Rahmat Ali took a deep breath and began: 'Ten years ago, I was a small-time gangster in Belgaum. I was just hitting the big-time when I was caught in a case of attempted murder and jailed. I had spent two years in prison when a young man named Hari Prasad became my cellmate. He was also in for attempted murder. I found out that his case was quite flimsy, it was clear that he had been framed...but that's a different story. Hari Prasad was a very intelligent young man, and although I didn't get along with him at first, I soon became very curious about the books that he constantly borrowed from the prison library and read. Hari was more then willing to share and soon, he opened up a world of knowledge to me—knowledge that, I was surprised to find, fascinated me. So much so that I wanted to formally educate myself while in prison. Although Hari Prasad himself did not seek formal education, he tutored me till I obtained a BSc degree. That changed my life, and I decided to give up the life of crime and walk the path of honesty.'

Virkar interrupted at this juncture. 'Look, we don't have time, so please come to the point.'

Rahmat Ali nodded and continued, 'Yes...yes. The prison

authorities noticed Hari Prasad's influence on me and began to direct other prisoners who were interested in being educated to him. Soon, Hari Prasad was given a small room in the hospital section of the prison where he conducted tuitions for students. He was also allowed to conduct experiments with chemicals found in the hospital as well as with herbs and plants grown around the prison area.'

Virkar tapped his feet, conveying his impatience. Rahmat Ali noticed this and quickened his pace. 'And then one day, a prisoner called Bhushan Hegde was brought into the prison. Apparently he had been treated at NIMHANS in Bangalore for some sort of a mental disorder. But it soon became obvious that he hadn't been cured. One day, in the prison hospital, Hegde attacked a fellow inmate with a blade and inflicted a deep wound. That inmate was HIV positive. Then with the same blade, now smeared with the blood of the HIV infected prisoner, he attacked two more persons, including a prison guard. He was finally subdued and thrown into the isolation cell, but the incident triggered a panic, as both the people attacked with the blood-smeared blade feared that they might have been infected with HIV.' Rahmat Ali paused to take a breath.

Raashi, who had been listening silently until now, broke into the conversation, 'Yes, I remember hearing about this case. But wasn't the prisoner transferred to a mental hospital?'

Rahmat Ali turned towards her and said, 'Yes, he was. But after six months he was sent back to Barudanga Prison. The same day, he attacked another inmate with a log of wood, hitting him on the head and sending him into coma.'

'What happened then?' Raashi asked.

'That night, Hari Prasad was called by the superintendent. When he came back, he was very disturbed. I asked him what had transpired in his meeting, but he didn't tell me. Three days later, Hegde was found dead. The official reason was given as food poisoning. But later that night, Hari Prasad broke down and told me that he had mixed some chemical that he had isolated from castor seeds into Hegde's food. He said that he had been promised two years off his sentence if he did so.'

Virkar butted in. 'But why ask Hari Prasad to get involved? People attack and kill each other in prisons regularly.'

Rahmat Ali smiled a rueful smile. 'Yes, they do, and our prison had become quite famous for that. Perhaps that's why they didn't want Hegde's death to catch any media attention. But there's no escaping that, is there?'

'And what about those people on the motorcycle today, why did they come for you?'

Rahmat smiled again. 'Apparently after you visited the prison this morning, they feared that I will tell you exactly what I'm telling you now.'

Virkar looked Rahmat Ali in the eyes and concluded that he was telling the truth. 'And what're you going to do now?'

'I'm going to disappear. And I advise you to do the same; they'll soon find you here, like I did.' And saying that, Rahmat Ali quickly turned and walked out of the door, leaving Raashi and Virkar staring at each other. Virkar waited for exactly three minutes before motioning to Raashi to walk into the small lobby with him. They paid their bill quickly and hailed a taxi all the way to the highway restaurant that Virkar had spotted earlier. Leaving Raashi seated in the midst of a group of travellers from Gujarat, Virkar went ahead and retrieved the Bullet from its hiding place. With Raashi riding pillion, Virkar finally opened up the Bullet's throttle on the highway and headed back towards Mumbai. It was only after they had covered around fifty kilometres that Virkar asked Raashi about her visit to the engineering college. She told him that she had got a copy of an old photograph, but more importantly, she had found information that conclusively pointed to Hari Prasad being the Compass Box Killer. The hostel warden at the boys' hostel had told Raashi that, while 'that foreigner lady' Tracy was alive, apart from paying his fees, she used to send some cash to Hari Prasad for his upkeep every few months. So as not to attract undue attention from the other students, she used to send the cash hidden inside an old, metal compass box.

37

Mumbai

They reached Mumbai in the early hours of the morning, delayed by the black, moonless night and a cloud cover that shut out even the meagre light of the stars. Given Virkar's night-riding skills, none of this would have mattered. But since he hadn't slept the past two nights, Virkar's body was battling with heightened exhaustion. He felt as though he was now heading straight into what marathon runners called 'The Wall': a physical state so debilitating that the body is forced to shut down operations till it has rested enough. Champion marathon runners train all year round to face 'The Wall', and yet many a time, when confronted by it, they have been known to collapse like a proverbial house of cards. But Virkar was not ready to collapse yet; the physical responsibility of Raashi sitting behind him on the Bullet was enough fuel in his body-tank to get them back to Mumbai safely.

As soon as they reached Raashi's Andheri flat, Virkar was ready to head off onwards to the Worli quarters of ACP Wagh, eager to share the details of his discovery of the Compass Box

Killer's identity, but on seeing his state, Raashi forced him to accompany her up to her flat. Virkar, too, realized that he needed rest purely to retain some kind of coherence in his thoughts, which were beginning to get muddled due to fatigue. He lay down on Raashi's soft bed, feeling the warmth engulf him immediately; within a few seconds, he was so fast asleep that he didn't even feel Raashi undo his boots and slip his clothes off his body.

The tittering of little children playing hide-and-seek finally woke Virkar up. He opened one eye and looked towards the window. It was still a little dark outside. He estimated that he might have slept for about half an hour or so. That was enough to give his muscles the rest they needed. He sat up and noticed that his clothes had been taken off him. Smiling to himself, he looked around, but Raashi was nowhere to be seen. He raised himself from the bed and padded barefoot to the bathroom, splashing water on his face at the washbasin. Now fully revived, he came back to the bedroom but still didn't find Raashi anywhere.

He walked into the hall, but that, too, was empty. Stepping into the kitchen that looked like it had not been used for a couple of days, he wondered if Raashi had gone to the shops across the road to pick up groceries. But something else was bothering him at the back of his head; he couldn't quite put a finger on it. He began to walk back to the bedroom when it suddenly struck him. It was the sound of children playing in the building compound. Children don't play in the morning; they go to school, unless it was the weekend, and this was not one. He quickly rushed to the window and looked down. The relaxed manner in which people were moving about did not resemble a Mumbai morning in the least.

He strode back into the bedroom and found his clothes neatly folded on a stool. His mobile phone was kept on top of the pile.

He snatched it up and checked the time: the digital clock read 6.30 p.m. Virkar slapped his forehead. It was evening. He had slept through the entire day. No wonder she wasn't around! He suddenly noticed that there were three missed calls from Raashi's number. He stabbed the redial button, but the phone kept ringing and she didn't answer. Scrolling through his contacts, he dialled ACP Wagh's number next. His call was picked up within two rings. 'Wagh saheb, I have to meet you immediately. I've made a very important discovery.'

From the other side, ACP Wagh spoke softly, 'Is that so? Then come immediately please, you're most welcome. I'm in the office.'

'Thank you, sir,' said Virkar, and hung up. For a second he wondered if there was a hint of sarcasm in ACP Wagh's tone, but then dismissed the thought. Deciding to waste no more time, Virkar slipped on his clothes and boots and rushed out of the apartment. Running down the stairs two at a time, he reached his parked Bullet within a few minutes and swung it towards the main road, hoping to make it to the Crime Branch headquarters within the hour.

He was successful; it was 7.30 p.m. when he knocked on ACP Wagh's door, seeking permission to enter. 'Come in, Virkar saheb, welcome,' called out ACP Wagh from inside. Virkar had been right—he could now not only hear the sarcasm in ACP Wagh's voice, but could see it plastered all over his face.

Feeling a little confused, Virkar blurted out the first thing that came to his mind. 'ACP saheb, I've discovered the identity of the Compass Box Killer.'

'Really?' asked ACP Wagh.

'Yes, sir, he is—'

'Hari Prasad from Belgaum,' cut in ACP Wagh, finishing Virkar's sentence. Virkar was stunned into silence. The dumbfounded look on his face must have registered with ACP Wagh, because he said, 'Wah! Virkar, that's a great performance.' He banged his hand on the steel call-bell on his table and the constable on duty popped his head inside immediately. Pointing at Virkar, ACP Wagh called out to the constable, 'Inspector saheb ke liye ek Oscar lao.'

'I... I...' stammered Virkar. The confused constable looked from Virkar to ACP Wagh, not knowing what to do. ACP Wagh was on a roll. He continued loudly in the same vein, 'Accha, Oscar nahi mila toh Screen ya Filmfare Award bhi chalega. Now go!' The constable saluted and left, still totally confused.

'ACP saheb, I don't know how you know...' managed Virkar in a weak voice.

'The same way the rest of the country knows, my friend,' the ACP retorted. He picked up a TV remote lying on his desk and switched the television on. Virkar turned to see Raashi on it say, 'This report was an exclusive brought to you by CrimeNews Channel. Once again, we would like to inform you that the Compass Box Killer, who has been identified as Hari Prasad, is roaming freely in Mumbai city. Please take a close look at his face again in the exclusive photograph brought to you by our channel.' The photograph that Raashi had got from Hari Prasad's engineering college flashed on the screen along with a morphed image of what a computer artist imagined him to look like at present. Virkar turned back towards the ACP and was about to convey his helpless indignation when he heard Raashi continue, 'The entire team at the CrimeNews Channel would like to thank Inspector Virkar of the Mumbai Crime Branch for his help in identifying the Compass Box Killer. We hope that his seniors at the Crime Branch value his contribution and begin the manhunt for Hari Prasad immediately.'

Virkar stared at the screen, dumbstruck.

ACP Wagh switched off the TV. 'So, Virkar, you've learned to play the media game. This, despite the fact that you are no longer on the case. I commend you on your shanpatti.'

'ACP saheb, aai chi shapat, I swear I didn't have anything to do with this. I was going to come to you directly from Belgaum but...'

'But what?'

Virkar fell silent. ACP Wagh shook his head. 'I've heard enough from you, Virkar, now you hear what I have to say.'

38

Virkar was standing on the jetty at Ferry Wharf waiting for the Koli Queen to dock. After a long time, he had felt the need to head out to sea armed with his favorite Jhinga Koliwada and half a crate of Godfather beer. ACP Wagh's 'words of wisdom' were still ringing in his ears and Virkar desperately needed to wash them down and spit them out of his system. The cool night breeze and the waves lapping the shore only made his thirst grow stronger. Suddenly, his mobile phone rang and perhaps because he was lost in his thoughts, he picked up the call without first checking the caller ID. From the other side, Raashi's voice said, 'They made me do it.'

'Who?' Virkar asked after a long pause.

'My bosses at the channel. You were fast asleep so I went to my office for a couple of hours. I was so thrilled with our breakthrough that I mistakenly blurted out to my boss that I had some exclusive news. They immediately forced me to break it live, even before my usual 9.00 p.m. slot. I tried to call and inform you a few times, but you didn't pick up.'

Virkar remembered seeing her missed calls but he didn't back down. 'You could have sent me a text to warn me.'

'I thought that by then you might be at your office. I had to go on air...'

Virkar cut the line, not wanting to hear any more. But suddenly he heard Raashi's voice call out from behind him, 'Is that how much you care for me, Virkar?' He spun around to see her standing on the dock about twenty feet away from him. Virkar remained silent, fuming. Raashi rushed up to him but on seeing his expression, she stopped short. In the light of the fluorescent tubes suspended on the pole behind him, Virkar saw the trickle of shiny tears on her cheek. Suddenly, Virkar felt a strong urge to drop the beer and the jhinga on to the dock and wrap his arms around Raashi, but he hesitated. She had done him wrong and he was going to make her pay for it.

'So what do you want?' he asked instead, infusing enough coldness in his voice to freeze the air between them.

'I... I... I want you to forgive me. I want us to get back together.'

'Is that really so?' asked Virkar. Behind him he could hear the sound of the Koli Queen docking at the jetty. An idea crept into Virkar's mind. 'What are you willing to do for that?'

Raashi swept a palm across her face, wiping her wet cheeks and revealing a cheeky smile underneath. 'Whatever you want me to do.' The twinkle in her eye said it all.

'I want you to wait right here, on this dock, till I come back.'

Raashi's smile vanished. Without another word, Virkar turned and jumped on to the deck of the Koli Queen docked behind him. He gave the signal for the boat to head out into the waters. Only when it was a few yards away from the jetty did Virkar turn around. Raashi looked as if her favorite toy had been snatched away from her. But she made no move to leave; she just stood there and watched as the Koli Queen made its way out into the open sea.

Virkar wrenched his mind away from Raashi and turned his entire attention to the job at hand—that of devouring the Jhinga Koliwada and chugging down the beer. A few mouthfuls later, he felt human again. A tinge of regret invaded his thoughts as the image of Raashi standing alone as the boat left the dock flashed before his eyes. But Virkar overcame this quickly as he remembered ACP Wagh steaming in his chair, screaming blue murder. He shook his head to wipe away all disturbing images and replaced them with the image of a blank blackboard. Then with an imaginary chalk he began to scribble points on the blackboard; important points related to the case on hand. He visualized the words T-r-a-c-y B-a-r-t-o-n and underneath that wrote 'killed/strangled, Smooth Operator'. Next to it, he mentally wrote down the names of Akurle, Bhandari and Colasco. On another side, he wrote the words C-o-m-p-a-s-s B-o-x K-i-l-l-e-r and under it wrote 'Hari Prasad, student, jail, life destroyed, used for murder, released from jail, decides to take revenge'. Then he mentally drew a line from there to the three names, completing the circle. On examining the circle inside his mind, Virkar realized that there was one link missing—the Smooth Operator. He had to be the person who had perpetrated the entire circle of deceit and revenge. He was to blame for the carnage at hand. It was not enough to catch Hari Prasad and end his killing spree; if true justice was to be served, the Smooth Operator, the man who had plotted it all, had to be brought to his knees and held responsible. He was still out there somewhere, hiding under layers of secrecy. Virkar had to peel away those layers and get to him before Hari Prasad did. Otherwise the injustice meted out to Hari Prasad would never surface. Virkar had to save Hari Prasad from himself, from his own actions. He had to save Hari Prasad from his revengeful alter ego, the Compass Box Killer.

Virkar sighed and looked up at the stars. He suddenly noticed that the Koli Queen had changed its course and was heading back to shore. Virkar had been so caught up in his thoughts that he had not realized that the boat had swung around. But he was quite sure that they had not been out for more than a couple of hours. He called out to the head boatman, 'Alfred mama, why've you turned back?' From his position at the head of the boat, Alfred Koli turned around and fixed a disparaging eye on Virkar. 'Because after eating so much of the jhinga, your brain has also turned into a jhinga.'

'What do you mean?' asked Virkar, puzzled.

'Arre melya, I just received a message on the boat's wireless radio that your girl has been standing in the same position at the dock for the past two hours.'

The Koli Queen reached Ferry Wharf in under thirty minutes. But even before the boat could be docked, Virkar had leapt off its prow on to the wharf and wrapped his arms around the still-waiting Raashi.

39

A live band struck up a tune from a corner of the upmarket nightclub. A beautiful female singer standing with the band picked up a mike and began to hum. A suave, well-groomed, young man wearing a finely tailored suit entered the nightclub. He walked with the assured gait of a predator through the maze of tables occupied by rich gentry. Some people seated at the tables nodded and smiled at him as he passed them and he smiled back in acknowledgement. At a corner table, two men wearing similarly expensive suits were deep in conversation about a big business deal. As he reached the table, they rose and shook his hand, asking him to join them. He flashed them a broad, winning smile and sat down. The female singer started to sing, 'Smooth operator…smoooth operator…'

'Huh!' exclaimed Virkar as he sat up on the bed, panting. He was naked and sweating. The dream that had woken him up was still playing in front of his eyes. He looked around and saw Raashi lying next to him. Her bare skin was shining in the soft glow of the orange sunrays streaming through the window. Virkar gulped a mouthful of air as he tried to calm his mind and pinpoint what it was about his dream that had woken him up. As he sat rewinding it in his mind's eye, Raashi stirred next to him. She propped herself up on one elbow and shot him a quizzical look. 'What's the matter?' she asked.

Virkar turned towards her. Looking straight into her bleary eyes, he said, 'I've got it.'

Raashi stifled a yawn, trying to rub the sleep out of her eyes. 'Got what?'

'The Smooth Operator is some sort of a rich businessman or industrialist with a sexual fetish.'

'What?' Raashi's eyes popped wide open.

'I couldn't put my finger on it before, but thanks to you, it's clear now.'

'Thanks to me?' she asked, confused.

'Well, yes. Thanks to you.'

Raashi opened her mouth to ask Virkar more questions but suddenly became aware of her nakedness. In a belated display of modesty, she pulled at the bedcover below them and wrapped it round her. Then, looking at Virkar with questioning eyes, she said, 'I have no idea what you're talking about.'

Virkar continued. 'Well, you told me about Sade's video of her song, *Smooth Operator*, and in Khandala, Bhoir told me that someone strangled Tracy with his bare hands, and that she had just consensual sex before she died. I had thought then that there was a connection between the two, but couldn't put my finger on it.'

Raashi rolled her eyes in exasperation. 'Sade… Bhoir… What am I missing? What's the link?'

'Erotic asphyxiation,' Virkar said slowly, emphasizing each word.

'Virkar, please speak plain English; it's too early in the morning for this.' Raashi couldn't help but show her irritation.

'It involves choking your sexual partner, thereby intentionally restricting oxygen to the brain, for sexual arousal,' Virkar explained.

'Have you totally lost it?' Gone was the vulnerability of the previous night; she was on edge now.

Virkar continued, 'It's a documented fact that people have indulged in erotic asphyxiation with their partners since ancient times. The arteries on both sides of the neck carry oxygen-rich blood from the heart to the brain and when these are compressed—as in the case of strangulation—the sudden loss of oxygen in the brain can increase sexual pleasure to supremely heightened levels. The high is said to be as potent as the one you get by doing cocaine.'

Raashi looked at Virkar with amazed eyes. 'Wow! And you figured all this out after a night with *me*.'

A blush rose to Virkar's cheeks. 'No, I learnt it in college. I'm a BA in psychology,' he said, a bit self-consciously.

'Hmm...you grow more and more interesting by the minute,' said Raashi, breaking the tension with her trademark smile. 'But I'm still unclear as to how you arrived at your conclusion.'

Virkar now launched into the details. 'Sometime back, I checked out the original music video of Sade's *Smooth Operator* and saw that the leading man was this rich, businessman type, fooling around with the singer. At one point he chases her up a building and attempts to strangle her with his bare hands. And then Bhoir told me that Tracy was strangled.'

Raashi cut in. 'But the title "Smooth Operator" has been given by Hari, the Compass Box Killer.'

'Exactly,' said Virkar. 'So I thought to myself, why would he use the title 'Smooth Operator' for the man? Why not not "Strangler" or "Choker" or something else? Was Hari into Sade's music? Then I realized that it was more likely that the name was given by Tracy to someone she was in a relationship with— perhaps because of her lover's sexual fetish.'

'But that doesn't make her lover a businessman or industrialist. He could just be some shady character,' said Raashi.

'Tracy, being the kind of woman she was, would not have got involved with a shady sort of man. She would be with someone suave and articulate like in the video—a businessman, a smooth operator.' Virkar paused and took a deep breath.

Raashi wasn't convinced. 'But, this erotic asfixi…asiation—I don't even know how to pronounce it! How does this come into the picture?'

'I think Tracy died while indulging in erotic asphyxiation during sexual intercourse with the Smooth Operator. There've been many cases of accidental deaths due to it. Most of them are among rich people who have alternative lifestyles and look for new ways of getting high. They explore different techniques for sexual arousal, trying to reach the ultimate orgasm, and sometimes they don't know when to stop,' Virkar explained.

Raashi scrunched up her face. 'I don't know. Your theory seems flimsy to me. There is no actual proof to draw such a conclusion.'

Virkar did not back down. 'The absence of proof does not mean that the hypothesis is wrong. It just means that the evidence needs to be found.'

'You'll be wasting your time proving your hypothesis while Hari Prasad kills another innocent man,' said Raashi, as she flounced off towards the bathroom with the bedsheet wrapped around her. Sitting naked on the bed, Virkar watched her go till she slammed the door behind her. Then Virkar went back into his thoughts. Was she right this time? Was he getting too carried away with this far-fetched theory? Was his desperation to crack the case clouding his judgement?

40

Look among the contributors to Slum Baalak Suraksha. The message was pithy and the handwriting was unmistakable. It was the Compass Box Killer again. However, this time the note was not written in blood but with a cheap ballpoint pen.

Virkar had found it folded and stuffed under the main door of his tenement at the police quarters in Bhoiwada. Written on a sheet of plain white paper, the note had been waiting for him at his doorstep when he had walked into his flat that morning, returning home after four days. Virkar read the note again with a magnifying glass. Reconfirming that the handwriting was identical to the earlier notes found at the crime scenes, his first instinct was to call ACP Wagh and inform him. But he held himself in check after the recent humiliation suffered at Wagh's hands.

But why did Hari Prasad send me this note? How do I find all the contributors to the NGO? Is this some bizarre way to make amends for all the atrocities he has committed? Or is he trying to mislead me into making a wrong move?

Virkar paced about his tiny living quarters, his mind racing. His thoughts went back to the earlier cryptic note inside the compass box in Barkat Alitronics: Three down. Now you'll have to work harder. Find the 'Smooth Operator' before I get to him. Virkar took a sharp breath. A sudden realization hit him like a sledgehammer. *Hari Prasad doesn't know who the Smooth Operator is. That's why he hasn't struck as yet after the last killing. But he obviously knows that the man is one of the financial contributors to Slum Baalak Suraksha. That's why he went to Advocate Shah, thinking that the NGO's lawyer would have the information. And now he wants me to help him out!*

Virkar sat down heavily on a chair. 'But as soon as he comes to know who the Smooth Operator is, he'll strike,' he muttered to himself.

He was still struggling with his theories when he reached the Crime Branch office that morning. He was torn between rushing off to investigate the clue in the note himself and sharing it with the new investigative team. But when he found that his name had not been included in the briefing note updating other officers on the Compass Box Killer case, all his doubts disappeared. This just made it easier on his conscience; Virkar now knew he was on his own.

Senior Inspector Sonavane, the new officer handling the case, obviously considered Virkar to be his rival—more so since Virkar had unearthed Hari Prasad's identity on his own while Inspector Sonavane had been rounding up the usual suspects. Virkar laughed to himself, wondering what Sonavane would say if he knew that Virkar had now been directly contacted by Hari Prasad, the Compass Box Killer, and given a lead! But Virkar decided not to share any information or theories with anyone till he had concrete proof.

Virkar was now on a mission to unearth the identity of the Smooth Operator. If his hunch was correct, the man called 'Smooth Operator' was a suave, moneyed man of some social standing with a sexual fetish. Since he didn't know how to begin looking for rich men into erotic fetishism, Virkar thought he'd begin by searching the Internet for businessmen and industrialists who might have been connected to Nigel Colasco.

Soon, however, Virkar discovered that Colasco had been a man about town when it came to his social connections. Search engines threw up photos of him with the city's top businessmen and socialites at various functions, award shows and product launches. Realizing that a cursory search of the Internet wouldn't turn up anything conclusive, he wondered whether he should pay Lourdes another visit. But he remembered that Lourdes' patience had worn thin the last time he had met her. She had also threatened to go to the Archbishop of Mumbai and complain about police harassment. Since Virkar was in enough trouble already, he decided against approaching her.

Virkar logged off his office computer and rose from his chair. He decided to pay the Slum Baalak Suraksha office another 'special' visit later that evening. With some amount of reluctance, he called Raashi and cancelled their rendezvous scheduled at her place that evening, citing overdue paperwork. She was a little upset at his abrupt behaviour, but when he rescheduled for the next evening promising a surprise, she grudgingly agreed.

As night fell, Virkar rolled down Mumbai's inky streets on his Bullet, making his way to Slum Baalak Suraksha's office. The wizened chowkidar saluted Virkar and wordlessly opened the gate. They were well acquainted with each other by now. After Colasco's death, when Virkar had surreptitiously visited his office the first time around, he had explained to the chowkidar that he was a friendly policeman on a secret personal mission to try and find Colasco's murderer. Although the chowkidar had no love for policemen, he had adored Colasco. Appreciating Virkar's earnestness, he had allowed him to enter the building to carry out his secret investigation in the hope that his erstwhile master may receive swift justice.

Within minutes, Virkar realized that he had been outsmarted by Inspector Sonavane's investigative team. They had seized all the files and computers from the office that now wore a threadbare look. Virkar kicked himself. He would have done the exact thing had he still been in charge of the case. Why hadn't he anticipated this in advance? Frustrated, he slammed the door behind him as he made his way out.

'What is the problem, saheb? Can I help?' the ever-eager chowkidar asked him as Virkar was leaving the premises.

Virkar managed a sarcastic laugh. 'Only if you have a list of all the rich people who gave money to Slum Baalak Suraksha.'

The sarcasm was lost on the old man who remained as earnest as ever. 'Where will a small person like me have such important information, saheb? But I'm sure Mr Gupte does.'

Virkar stopped in his tracks. 'Mr Gupte?'

'Our accountant, saheb,' explained the chowkidar. 'He was away at his native place in Bhandara for the past month and returned just this morning.'

Virkar was in two minds whether to go up to Gupte's home right then or wait till the morning. Gupte was a family man, and families are known to get extremely disturbed when policemen knock on their doors late at night. But the chowkidar, who seemed to know a lot, informed him that Gupte's wife and daughters were still away in Bhandara, and Gupte was busy at play. Lowering his voice to a conspiratorial tone, he said, 'Saheb, sometimes Gupte saheb goes to the Samrat Social Club in Kurla.'

'And how do you know that? Did you go there with him?'

'No, no, saheb. I'm a God-fearing man. But occasionally the

local taxi drivers who dropped him there turned out to be from my part of the country,' he smiled slyly.

As he rode off, Virkar couldn't help laughing to himself, amazed at the quantum of information the chowkidar had. 'God help those who get on the wrong side of a Mumbai chowkidar!' he said to himself.

It was almost midnight by the time Virkar reached the Samrat Social Club. It was just another one of the several illegal gambling joints that had sprung up across Mumbai under the guise of legally licensed 'card rooms'. But Virkar was in no mood to raid the place, so he politely asked the guards standing outside to summon the owner.

'Look, I don't want to disturb your business. I just want to speak to a man called Gupte,' Virkar explained when the owner came out to meet him.

The owner, however, looked extremely unwilling to help. 'I have two ACPs and three Inspectors playing Rummy inside,' he proudly announced to Virkar.

'Good. Then they'll surely come out and help you when I shoot you in your leg,' said Virkar, casually stroking his Browning 9mm service revolver that he had tucked into his waistband. Suddenly, the owner's attitude underwent a sea change. Within five minutes, two muscle-bound men escorted out a trembling, bespectacled, ratty-looking man. Virkar was a little amused to notice the resemblance Gupte had to cartoonist R. K. Laxman's caricature of the 'common man'. He motioned for Gupte to sit behind him on the Bullet, and without speaking to him at all, rode all the way back to Gupte's building. By this time, Gupte was almost on the verge of a breakdown. Virkar let him sweat for a while, and only after he had been ushered inside Gupte's second-floor flat did Virkar finally speak.

'Who are the contributors to the Slum Baalak Surakasha?'

'The money comes in through corporate sources,' Gupte blurted without hesitation.

'Who are these corporate sources?' Gupte shivered but kept quiet. Virkar sighed. He looked towards a family photograph in which a smiling Gupte was pictured with his wife and two little daughters.

'Have your wife and daughters ever been to the Samrat Social Club?' Virkar asked casually.

Without wasting another moment, Gupte said, 'It's a Trust funded by many leading corporates of Mumbai. It's administered by CorpsRam—the Corporate Social Responsibility Association of Mumbai.'

'Who is in charge of this...CorpsRam?'

'Vasant Dixit.'

'Who...the man who owns Dixitel?' asked Virkar surprised.

'Yes.'

Gupte had just named the man known in the media as the 'telecom king' of India.

Virkar felt a strange buzzing in his brain. 'The telecom king,' he muttered out loud. His mind instinctively began using the technique that used word associations to enhance creativity and cognition—a technique he had learned in his psychology course.

Nèw words began to tumble about in his brain.

Telecom King...Telephone King...Telephone Operator...Smooth Operator.

41

There are no tigers left in the forests surrounding the Gadchiroli district in interior Maharashtra. But till the middle of the last century, it had, perhaps, the biggest tiger population in the country. Tiger hunting was still legal then and the Madia tribe of the area had a unique technique of driving the animal of out of its hidden lair in the jungle. The technique was known as 'haaka'. The tribals gathered up all the metal kitchen utensils in their homes and walked through the jungle clanging them against each other. The loud din created by metal upon metal shocked the tiger into believing that a hunting party was approaching. Fearing for its life, the tiger would run in the opposite direction, straight into the arms of the actual hunting party that was approaching from the other side. During his tenure in Gadchiroli, Virkar had learnt about this technique while scouring the jungle, hunting Maoists along with the tribals. Today, however, he was going to use the haaka in an entirely new way—to flush out a different kind of tiger: one who was not a man-eater, but was equally powerful and dangerous.

Virkar, dressed in a smart shirt and trousers that made him look less like a policeman and more like a mid-rung corporate climber, was standing across the road from the shiny glass multi-story building which housed Dixitel's global headquarters in the Bandra Kurla Complex. In his head, Virkar had been toying with various ideas that would help him get to the eighteenth-floor office of Vasant Dixit. Ultimately, he had settled upon using his own version of the haaka.

Taking a deep breath, he walked into the shining marble lobby and went straight to the large reception area that was stylishly placed right in the centre of the lobby.

'I'd like to meet Mr Vasant Dixit, please,' he told the smart young receptionist.

The woman looked him up and down and said, 'Mr Dixit is busy. Is there anyone else I could connect you with?'

Virkar nodded. 'You could connect me to his personal secretary.'

The receptionist flashed him a tiny smile. 'Sure, let me just check. And may I know where you've come from?'

'I've come from the Christian Cemetery in Khandala. I have a message for Mr Dixit from one of its occupants,' said Virkar.

The receptionist looked at him quizzically. She punched some number on the console in front of her and spoke into the telephone in an undertone. Cupping her hand on the receiver, she looked at Virkar. 'May I know what your message is?' Virkar cracked an enigmatic smile. 'It's only for Mr Dixit's ears.' The receptionist rolled her eyes and repeated Virkar's words to the person on the other end of the line. She replaced the receiver and motioned Virkar towards the lift on the far side of the lobby. 'Please take the lift to the eighteenth floor. Mr Dixit's personal assistant will meet you there,' she said.

Virkar smiled to himself as he went through the security check before taking the lift. It seemed he had misjudged the situation. The man he had thought to be a tiger had turned out to be a jackal. Virkar rode the lift to the eighteenth floor and was greeted right outside the lift by a young, suited, Parsi man who looked as if he had just stepped out of a Page 3 party. 'I'm Hozi Sethna, Mr Dixit's personal assistant. And I didn't catch your name?'

'My name is not important,' said Virkar, 'where I've come from, is.'

'Right. And you've come from some Christian cemetery in Khandala, and you have a message for Mr Dixit?'

'Yes,' said Virkar.

'Okay, so what is the message?'

'The message is only for Mr Dixit.'

'Look, Mr Cemetary, Mr Dixit is busy. Give me the message and I'll make sure it reaches him.'

'This is too personal.'

Sethna gave Virkar a condescending smile. 'I know all the personal details of Mr Dixit.'

'Do you know about his sexual fetishes too?' asked Virkar nonchalantly. 'Then I don't have a problem telling you. But if you don't, better get me to him fast. I'm busy too, so don't waste my time.'

Hozi Sethna's creamy skin turned red. He excused himself and walked away, letting Virkar stand by himself next to the lift. Five minutes later, he was back with two huge men dressed in dark safari suits. The two safari-suited men fell in step on either side of Virkar.

Hozi Sethna looked at the man in the safari suit on Virkar's left. The look was enough for the man to clamp down a heavy hand on Virkar's shoulder. Virkar realized that he had just a few seconds left. Suddenly he sat down on his haunches, breaking free from the man's grasp. Swivelling, Virkar jabbed out with his right hand. His knuckles connected with the safari-suited man's testicles. A strangled sound escaped the man's lips as he crashed down to his knees, holding his prized possessions. Safari suit number two had by now unleashed a kick towards the crouched Virkar. The kick was intended to connect with Virkar's jaw, but Virkar had anticipated this. He thrust his hand upwards, connecting with the man's calf and using the momentum of the kick to push the leg further along its path till it went past his chin. Finding nothing to connect with, the kick shot out in the blank air, making Safari suit number two lose his balance. His other leg, too, flew out from under him and with a thud, he landed on his backside. Virkar knew that he would spring up in no time, so before the fallen man could gather himself, Virkar stabbed Safari suit number two's throat with his right knee.

Leaving Safari suit number two gagging on the floor next to his colleague, Virkar stood up and faced a cringing Hozi Sethna. 'I know that Vasant Dixit paid off Colasco, Akurle and Bhandari. He's the next target of the Compass Box Killer. Tell him that I know of a way that can save him.'

Hozi Sethna stood frozen, but before Virkar could say anything else, a door to his right burst open and half a dozen similar-looking, safari-suited men rushed towards him. Virkar knew he was outnumbered. In a menacing tone, he said, 'If they touch me, I'll...'

He did not have to complete his sentence. Hozi Sethna raised his hand and the safari-suited men stopped in their tracks. 'Please escort him outside this building politely. And make sure he never comes back,' he said, betraying no emotion. The safari-suited men fell in double formation around and behind Virkar, forcing him to walk out of the office towards the elevator. As he rode down the elevator to the lobby surrounded by the guards, Virkar smiled to himself. An amusing phrase popped into his head: 'Haaka laga dhandhe pe, sher aaya phande mein.' His strategy was working; the quarry had walked into the trap.

42

'In Breaking News today, we bring to you one of the most bizarre acts of police intimidation ever seen,' Raashi's voice speaking in her familiar shrill tones pierced through Virkar's thoughts, snapping him to attention.

He had been lying on the sofa in front of his television, flipping through channels as he passed the time. After he had left the Dixitel headquarters, the first thing he did was to call Raashi's mobile phone. When she hadn't answered, he had sent her a text, asking her to call him back. Making his way back to his office, he had shuffled papers on his desk, pretending to be busy while, in fact, his mind was racing, thinking of every possible outcome of his move to buttonhole Vasant Dixit. As evening came around, he made his way back to his quarters. There he showered and then sat down in front of the television. As 9.00 p.m. drew close, he switched to the CrimeNews Channel for the prime time news update.

Now he stared stonily as Raashi's sombre face appeared on the screen. 'Crime Branch Officer, Inspector Virkar, today assaulted two personal bodyguards of respected industrialist Vasant Dixit.' The screen cut to grainy CCTV footage showing Virkar attacking the two safari-suited security men in Dixitel's office. Raashi's voice continued to speak over the visuals. 'Sometime earlier this morning, Inspector Virkar, who has clearly become unstable after he was removed from the Compass Box Killer case, entered the headquarters of Dixitel and demanded ten lakh rupees to settle a drummed-up case connected to Mr Vasant Dixit's Khandala bungalow.'

On the screen, Virkar could see himself in the lobby of Dixitel's headquarters talking to the receptionist. His voice was muffled and the only words that were clear were 'from… Khandala…occupants there.' A concerned-looking Raashi came back on the screen. 'Inspector Virkar was invited up to meet Mr Dixit's personal assistant to sort out the misunderstanding. Once there, he assaulted Mr Dixit's personal bodyguards. Had it not been for the restraint shown by Mr Hozi Sethna, Mr Dixit's P.A., his bodyguards would surely have retaliated. But, in an attempt to avoid any embarrassment to the Mumbai police, Mr Sethna patiently asked his guards to escort Inspector Virkar out of his premises.'

The screen cut to grainy footage of Hozi Sethna asking his guards to politely walk Virkar out of the building. Raashi, now back on the screen, dealt the final blow. 'Are the authorities going to take note of this kind of behaviour? If important people like Mr Vasant Dixit can be treated with such disdain, what can we expect for the common man? Where does he stand? We posed this question to both the Home Minister and the Police Commissioner, but they remained unavailable for comment. We shall wait for them to become available. And if they don't, we will go to their houses and demand an answer.'

Virkar smiled to himself. He had been expecting this. The previous day, while researching Vasant Dixit's background on the

Internet, he had come across a news item that had detailed all his holdings and properties. Along with the fact that he owned a palatial bungalow in Khandala, there was also a small mention of the fact that Vasant Dixit was a non-active majority stakeholder of a broadcast company that owned a bouquet of channels. One of them happened to be CrimeNews Channel.

As soon as he came to know this fact, he had made the connection. He had realized that Raashi had been playing him all along—at Vasant Dixit's behest. She had met him at the Sunny Bar to try and find out how much he knew, but by mistake had let slip Smooth Operator's connection to the Sade video. To rectify her mistake, she had followed Virkar to Khandala to find out what he was up to. As he got closer to the truth, she had enticed him into opening up to her completely so that he would take her along with him to Belgaum. He felt specially cheated by the way she had made the Hari Prasad story public to draw away attention from the Smooth Operator. Virkar had grown suspicious immediately, but she had distracted him once again—although not enough to put all his doubts to rest.

Virkar lay back on the sofa. After watching Raashi's show, the huge weight of his suspicions having been confirmed finally hit him smack on his chest. The sting of the betrayal rose within him and made its way to his eyes. But Virkar fought back. In an attempt to sweep aside the anger and hurt, he focused on how foolish he had been. He had let his guard down and let himself be manipulated. He had allowed Raashi to exploit his vulnerability. She had realized that, apart from the physical intimacy, he also needed the companionship that she had begun to provide. He had been fooled into believing, at least for a while, that her reciprocation was real—something that normally would not have happened had it not been for the fact that Raashi had made him…feel. She had made him feel his emotions and his loneliness.

The shrill ring of his mobile phone disturbed his thoughts. Virkar took the call, only to hear a terse command from ACP Wagh.

'Report to the Additional Commissioner's office tomorrow at 9.00 a.m.'

43

She was waiting for him in the corridor, pretending to be deep in conversation with a senior police officer that Virkar didn't know.

He had just finished meeting with the Additional Commissioner of Police, Abhinav Kumar, and was headed down the corridor, mulling over his next course of action. Abhinav Kumar had informed him that Vasant Dixit was slapping a hundred crore rupees defamation suit on the police department because of Virkar's actions. Virkar had quickly examined all future courses of action and realized that not only was his current position in the Crime Branch threatened, but his entire career had come under a cloud. He had expressed his regrets for putting the police department in such a situation and sought permission to personally apologize to Vasant Dixit and request him to withdraw the defamation case. Although his suggestion was unorthodox, Abhinav Kumar had agreed to arrange a meeting so that Virkar could tender his formal apology and request Dixit to withdraw the case and save the police department the bad publicity.

Out in the corridor, he came upon Raashi so suddenly that he didn't have any time to react, let alone to take any evasive action to avoid her. He was forced to stop in front of her as she was blocking the corridor, purposely placing herself in such a position that it would seem very odd if he were to walk around her without acknowledging her at all.

'Hello,' he said, as non-committal as ever.

'Hi, Virkar,' she said, breaking into a broad, toothy smile. The senior police officer with her looked at Virkar and realized that his time with her was up and he should move on, giving way to his junior.

For a few seconds they stood awkwardly together, trying to avoid any eye contact. It was Raashi who, as usual, broke the silence.

'Why haven't you been answering my calls?'

Virkar replied with a dry grunt of laughter. Raashi didn't react but continued, 'I have some explaining to do.'

Virkar's laugh grew sharp, now mixed with a hint of sarcasm. Raashi spoke in a tone that sounded hopeful: 'I know I've said this to you before, but you have to understand. It's not personal.'

'Oh, yes, it is!' exploded Virkar, speaking for the first time. Letting the sarcasm flow into his voice, he said, 'It's all for *your* personal growth.'

Raashi's dilated pupils contracted a little in response to this statement, but the hopeful twinkle refused to lose its sparkle. 'I'm an ambitious woman. Surely you understand that?'

Virkar retorted, 'Correction. You're a *cut-throat* ambitious woman and I do understand that.'

'I'm as cut-throat as you are, Virkar,' said Raashi, her tone now matter-of-fact. 'Don't pretend like you wouldn't do anything to further your career. You're desperate to catch the Compass Box Killer and the Smooth Operator so that you win a medal… or get a promotion. Isn't that right?'

Virkar looked surprised. 'Is that what you think I've been doing all this time?'

Raashi was unmoved. 'Why else? I can see no other reason.'

Virkar spoke through clenched teeth, 'Maybe I still believe in the triumph of good over evil. That there is a right and a wrong—'

Raashi cut him off. 'Oh, come now, Virkar, let's go home to my place. I'll listen to your bhaashan between my bedsheets.'

Virkar's dry laugh was back again. Only this time, it was accompanied by a vigorous shake of his head as if he was desperately trying to dislodge the incredulous feeling that was stuck between his ears. 'You will go far, very far, without ever looking back,' he said, finally.

Raashi didn't say anything; she just stared at Virkar, her face hardening. Virkar turned to go, but then, as if he had remembered something, he turned back. Looking directly into Raashi's eyes, he said, 'Well, maybe you'll look back some day on your way down, only to see the bodies of the people that you have trampled over on your journey upwards. But isn't it a sad thing that they all would be lying by the wayside and there would be no one to catch you when you're falling?'

Raashi stood silent, a glazed look in her eyes. Virkar finally turned and walked away from her. He could feel her eyes boring holes into his back as he walked down the corridor.

Stepping around the corner, he quickly cut across the compound and walked towards an unmarked, white, windowless van parked on the far corner. Casting furtive glances all around to make sure that he wasn't being watched, he knocked on the side panel of the van. The panel slid open to show an array of digital recording equipment that was arranged on a counter inside. Two men wearing headphones sat on tiny stools working on the dials and knobs of the equipment. Virkar stepped inside and the panel slid shut behind him.

Across the compound, Raashi watched the van from a position behind a pillar in the corridor. A few seconds later, she turned around and receded down the corridor in the opposite direction.

44

'There will be a white, windowless van positioned somewhere close by that will be recording everything you say,' she said.

Vasant Dixit laughed his throaty, sexy laugh. 'How old school is that? That kind of surveillance went away along with the nineties.'

Raashi shrugged. 'What can you expect? The Mumbai police don't have the budget to keep up with the times.'

Vasant Dixit smiled. 'Sweetheart, even if they *had* the budget, they couldn't compete with me. I mean...my company supplies them with surveillance equipment, for God's sake. How foolish is that guy?'

Raashi shrugged again. 'He is the biggest fool of them all.' They were sitting in a glass-fronted room of Vasant Dixit's Madh Island bungalow that overlooked the flat expanse of Dana Pani Beach.

Madh Island is not really an island but a cluster of old-world fishing villages and farmlands nestled cozily on the northwest shoreline of suburban Mumbai. Lavish bungalows owned by members of the upper echelons of Mumbai line its serene beaches. It can be accessed by road via the Mumbai suburb of Malad or by taking a ferry across from the fishing village in Versova. However, due to its proximity and an impressive multiple-beach shoreline, it is favoured by all stratas as a picnic destination. The super-rich organize private parties in their lavish, landscaped bungalows while the not so well-heeled rent out beachfront shacks by the hour and engage in wanton drinking, dancing and frolicking on the seashore.

Vasant Dixit's massive, super-posh bungalow across the flat Dana Pani Beach was sprawled across five acres of the sloping hilly land facing west. Perched on a flat piece of land in the middle of the slope, the bungalow housed seven sea-facing bedrooms, a ballroom-sized living room, a swimming pool and a tennis court. Right outside the massive front door, two huge party lawns had been carved out of the slope and extended like giant green steps down to the ten-foot-high boundary wall that surrounded the property and touched the road running along the beach. Behind the bungalow, to the east, the hilly portion of the land sloped up through a wooded area all the way up to the main road that ran through the island. Three steel TV towers stood like sentinels on three corners of the bungalow walls, and in the fourth corner to the south, a massive rock face rose out of the hill and completed the fortress-like picture of the bungalow. Large steps had been carved into the rock face leading to a flat, bald tabletop outcrop that was the highest beachfront point on Madh Island. The view from the outcrop was magnificent as directly across it lay the sparkling blue sea. On a clear day, one could see all the way to Uttan Lighthouse in the north and Prong's Lighthouse in Colaba, the southernmost tip of Mumbai.

'You've done well, babes,' smiled Vasant Dixit, trailing his index finger along her cheek. 'You're on the fast track. Just make sure that you keep your eyes on your goal. At all times.'

Raashi nodded. 'What will you do to him?' she asked, her expression conveying nothing.

Vasant Dixit gave her a long look. 'You like him, don't you?'

'No! I was just asking out of academic curiosity,' Raashi protested.

'Hmm,' said Vasant Dixit, looking out over the sea at the few fishing boats making their way towards the shallow waters. 'I'll probably have him posted to some small mofussil town where he'll disappear into oblivion.'

Raashi looked unsure. 'If I may say something… I'd like to warn you that this one is not entirely easy to get rid of.'

Vasant Dixit smiled. 'See, I *knew* that you thought highly of him.'

'Well, I would not underestimate him as an opponent, that's all I meant to say.'

'My dear girl, why do you underestimate me?'|

Raashi backtracked at once. 'Oh no, Mr Dixit, I don't underestimate you at all.'

But Vasant Dixit's dark eyes were as shiny as fresh coal. 'Do you think that a man of limited intelligence and influence would have been able to cover up the murder of a young, white woman? You know how many layers of subterfuge I created? Do you know how I arm-twisted Colasco into disposing off Tracy's body and keeping mum about this for nine years? The greedy sucker kept quiet about the death of someone he considered a good friend because I threatened to stop funding Slum Baalak Suraksha. I had his balls in my fist. He was so shit scared of me that he even went to his grave without giving an inkling of my involvement in the case. I'll never be connected with the crime.'

Sweat broke out on Raashi's brow. She never failed to be intimidated by Vasant Dixit although she had belonged to his inner circle for some time now. She had been handpicked from the team of management trainees at Dixitel and placed at the CrimeNews Channel as a likely contender for its future boss. Her ambitious streak was something that Vasant Dixit had identified early on and fuelled from time to time, to the point that she was now in over her head in the cover-up of a murder he had committed.

'They'll never be able to prove it,' Dixit hissed through clenched teeth. 'Never be able to connect it with me. Do you know why?' His smile was sinister. 'Because I made everyone an accessory. If I went down, they would go down with me. Do you understand?'

Raashi nodded mutely, her heart thumping.

But Vasant Dixit did not let up. 'No, I don't think you understand. Let me illustrate with an example. Let's take you for instance. If you were to tell anyone what I'm telling you now, do you know what will happen?' Raashi didn't have to reply, Vasant Dixit continued, 'They would find you guilty of abetment. Of abetting me in my quest to cover up my involvement, you would be found guilty of criminal conspiracy—of conspiring with me to actively mislead Virkar and impede an investigation.'

Raashi shook her head vigorously from side to side. 'But, Mr Dixit, I'll never go against you. I'm your most trusted person.'

Vasant Dixit's smile now chilled Raashi to the bone. 'I'm glad to hear you say that, because if I had any doubts about it, the cameras planted in your apartment and within this room will provide enough evidence of the same to the police.'

Raashi was tongue-tied; she opened her mouth to say something, but no sound came out. Vasant Dixit looked at her intently; a wave of amusement now washed away his earlier expression. He seemed to return to his former genial self at once.

'Don't worry, babes, that day will never come. Now relax.'

He reached out to pick up a small but powerful digital handycam lying on a table, and handed it to her. 'Here. I'm sure you know how to operate this. Get some good footage of the party outside.'

Raashi regained her composure, grabbed the camera, nodded and turned to leave. As she was about to exit, Vasant Dixit called out from behind her, 'Just a second… What's his favourite drink?'

Raashi turned and smiled. 'This one's not going to be so easy, even for you!'

45

Virkar sat on a wooden bench atop the flat outcrop of land on the premises of Vasant Dixit's bungalow. He had arrived at the gates at four o'clock sharp, the stipulated time given to him for his meeting with the man of the hour. Having been led in by the grey safari-suits through a side entrance, he had been thoroughly searched for any concealed weapons. When the safari-suits were satisfied, they had led him to the tabletop and asked him to sit on the bench and wait. Smiling to himself, he had sat looking out towards the sea. A couple of fishing boats, busy casting their nets in the shallow waters bobbed right across from him in the sea. He felt as if he was in a smuggler's adda straight out of a Hindi film from the seventies. It had now been two hours since he had arrived and he had gotten restless. He stood up and stretched, casually walking over to the edge of the tabletop. The safari-suits eyed him but made no move to stop him. Walking to the western side of the outcrop, Virkar looked down and saw an amazing scenario.

In the two bungalow lawns below and by the poolside, little children ran helter-skelter, chased by their mothers and the maids who took care of them. Multi-coloured balloons were everywhere—spread across the lawns, floating in the swimming pool, hung from every corner jutting out of the bungalow. Small, air-filled dinghy boats plied in the swimming pool with little children as passengers screaming their lungs out in sheer joy. A massive inflated balloon-slide transported older children into the pool from a height of about twenty feet. An inflated balloon-castle stood on one side of the lawn, inviting little children to run in and out of its open doors. As if this was not enough, men dressed as clowns handed out helium gas-filled balloons and other goodies to the little children as soon as they expressed laughter, anger, hunger or any other emotion. To Virkar, who was surveying the scene from the tabletop, which was at a height of more than 100 metres, the little children down below looked like colourful ants cavorting between colourful ant eggs.

A coarse hand on Virkar's shoulder pulled him out of his thoughts. He turned to see one of the grey suits signalling him back to the bench. 'Please be seated. Boss will be here in a few minutes.'

Without any protest, Virkar walked back to the bench. A slight movement at the corner of his eye caught his attention. Virkar turned to see Vasant Dixit, a middle-aged, well-groomed man dressed in casual chinos and a polo T-shirt walk up the rock stairs. Virkar recognized him from the countless images he had seen of the man in the media. As Vasant Dixit walked towards him, Virkar noticed a plume of smoke emanating from his mouth—only then did he notice the cigar in the businessman's hand. The two men walking behind Vasant Dixit were dressed in fawn-coloured safari suits. Virkar guessed that they were servers instead of bodyguards because of the folding chair and table that they carried in their hands along with the ice box that they were lugging.

Vasant Dixit walked up to Virkar, who rose from the bench and held out his hand. But Vasant Dixit only stuck the cigar in his mouth and motioned for him to sit down. Virkar sat down on the bench again. The two servers unfolded the table and chair in front of him. Placing the ice box next to the table, they opened it and drew out a crystal beer mug and a chilled bottle of Godfather beer. Virkar eyed the bottle and then shot a glance towards Vasant Dixit. The man was not looking at him but at the Rolex on his wrist. By this time, the servers had finished pouring the beer into the crystal mug. Plugging the open neck of the bottle with the bottle stopper, they receded into the background. Vasant Dixit finally took the cigar out of his mouth and flicked the ash on to the ground. With an amused expression, he looked Virkar straight in the eye and said, 'Please, drink! This is your favourite beer, isn't it? I had to send a man all the way to Versova for it. Even then it took him time to find it—it's so bloody rare.'

Virkar did not make a move to pick up the beer mug. He opened his mouth to say something, but Vasant Dixit raised his hand to silence him. Breaking into a smile that did not reach his eyes, he said, 'If we're going to be friends, shouldn't we drink together?'

Virkar remained expressionless. 'But where is your drink, Mr Dixit?'

Vasant Dixit smiled again. 'Ah, good point! You see, I'm not drinking just yet; I have to go down and play with my five-year-old son. It's his birthday and we're having a party, as you may have seen.'

Virkar's voice remained as flat as before. 'Oh, so your son was born four years after you killed Tracy Barton?'

Vasant Dixit's eyes went ice cold but the smile remained intact. 'Inspector Virkar, I thought you had come here to apologize, but I can see that there is no change in your attitude.'

Virkar's voice hardened. 'It's difficult to change an attitude, don't you agree, Mr Dixit? No matter how much you change, you're always going to remain a killer. Isn't that so?'

Vasant Dixit stared at Virkar with an intensity that threatened to burn a hole into Virkar's skull. Finally he broke into a dry laugh. 'What do you want from me? An admission of guilt? Okay, chalo, I confess. I killed her. But it was an accident.'

'Acchha, an accident?' Virkar sneered

'Yes,' said Vasant Dixit, 'an accident, a sexual accident.'

Virkar shot back, 'You put your hands around her throat and choked the life out of her and you call it an accident?' The veins in his temples were throbbing.

'Believe me, Inspector, I didn't mean to kill her. I liked her—'

Virkar cut him off. 'You liked her enough to pay off three people to cover up her death and have her buried in a godforsaken part of earth, forgotten away.'

'Well, what else was I supposed to do? Who cares about these hippy-charsi phirangs anyway? They are screwing themselves up with drugs and sex anyway, right? Who gives a damn about them?'

It was Virkar's turn to laugh. 'Well, guess what Mr Dixit? You chose the wrong phirang to kill. Somebody did care about this particular hippy. He has already killed the three men you paid to cover up the murder, and now he's coming for you.'

Vasant Dixit drew on his cigar. Letting the plume of smoke curl out of his mouth, he smiled. 'Look around you; does it look like anyone can get to me?'

Virkar laughed again. 'A determined killer can get to even kings and prime ministers, and you're just a man with a lot of money. He will get to you, it's only a matter of time. No one can save you.'

Vasant Dixit got up all of a sudden, anger flashing in his eyes. 'No one can save *you* now, Inspector. Your job is gone. Your career is gone. It's all over for you.'

'We'll see about that,' Virkar replied, a slight smile lingering on his face.

Vasant Dixit smiled back. 'You think you're so smart, don't you?' He looked towards the safari-suits. Two men sprang from both sides of Virkar and ripped his shirt off his body. Reaching under his armpit, they pulled out a taped mini transmitter. Flinging it on to the ground, one of the safari-suits crushed it under his foot.

Vasant Dixit now spoke in a voice that was calm and composed, 'You think that recording device in your armpit was transmitting down to the van that's standing on the road behind the bungalow. Well, think again! Why do you think I called you here to meet me? Look around you. You see those towers? They have the most sophisticated radio wave jamming devices in the world. They can intercept and scramble any signal being transmitted towards the road. I'm not called the telecom king of India for nothing.'

Virkar stared at him mutely. 'You had your fun, but, Inspector, the real fun begins now. Goodbye,' he sneered before turning and walking away.

Virkar stood by the bench watching him disappear. He was not bothered about the transmitter that had been found, but was wondering if the tiny microchip transmitter, the one stuck below his testicles, had transmitted everything clearly to Alfred Koli's radio transmitter aboard the Koli Queen that was anchored in the sea right across from the bungalow, pretending to be fishing in the waters.

46

'Today, I'm the happiest man alive,' Vasant Dixit's voice boomed out over the lawns through the speakers that were strategically placed in various corners. He was standing with a mike in his hand on a small stage that was adorned with human-sized balloons and set up at the head of the main lawn.

After leaving Virkar at the tabletop, he had made his way down the stone steps and waded through the sea of balloons and children to finally reach his five-year-old son. The child was in his gorgeous wife's arms, enjoying all the attention that was being lavished on him. Virkar was being led by the safari-suits down from the tabletop and towards the side entrance. But on hearing their master's voice over the loudspeaker, the safari-suits had instinctively stopped and were staring in the direction of the small stage. On the stage, Vasant Dixit was a picture of a perfect happiness. He hardly looked like a man who had just had an altercation with a police officer who had accused him of murder—or like a man who had admitted to it. Instead, he was looking like a man who was having a truly great day. Virkar, too, stood and watched him as he continued to speak, 'My son, Ved—Vedanta Dixit—has turned five today, and I'm so glad that you are all here to share this special day with him.' A huge wave of applause erupted across the lawn as the children and their minders expressed their appreciation. 'And now, I have a special song that I want to sing for my little Vedster,' said Vasant Dixit. The excitement in his voice was palpable and the safari-suits around Virkar smiled as they watched their boss, waiting for his special song.

Boxed in by the safari-suit squad Virkar resigned himself to watching Vasant Dixit's act.

With a theatrical flourish, Vasant Dixit dropped his cigar on to the stage and stubbed it out to the accompaniment of giggles and titters. Then, taking a deep breath, he launched into a rendition of the 'Happy Birthday' song.

But as soon as he began to sing, one of the life-sized balloons hanging above him burst, showering him with glittering confetti. Vasant Dixit was surprised, but on hearing the excited applause of the little children, he continued gamely. His singing now seemed to only favour the high tones. The claps and exclamation from the children grew as his voice took on a squeaky tone. Vasant Dixit now sounded as if he was doing a Donald Duck impression. 'May you have many more...' he squeaked in a high-pitched voice. The laughter around him was loud and rampant. As if on cue, two huge, life-sized balloons burst on either side of him, showering him with a thousand more confetti strips. The claps got louder and more reverberating. The appreciation of his funny act was universal. The serious-looking safari-suits, too, turned into tittering idiots. The crowd joined in a high-pitched chorus to accompany Vasant Dixit's squeaky singing. 'Happy birthday, dear Vedanta... Happy birthday toooo youuuu...' As the last notes subsided, Vasant Dixit grabbed his throat and started gagging, as if tired by all the high-pitched singing. Laughter and claps rose to thunderous levels. The crowd gathered around had obviously never seen Vasant Dixit in such a sporting mood. He was really milking the moment for whatever it was worth. The crowd watched in merriment as Vasant Dixit fell to his knees, continuing his gagging act, and everyone clapped even harder as he sprawled on the floor of the stage, pretending to be exhausted by his Donald Duck impression. The safari-suits, too, nudged each other in appreciation of their boss's talent.

Suddenly, a scream rent the air. Vasant Dixit's wife had gone up on stage to bring her husband down for the cake-cutting ceremony. But despite her calling out to him, he had not stirred and lain still. She had shaken him, clasping his hand in hers. When she attempted to pull him up gently, his hand slipped out of hers and rolled to the side, hitting the floor with a thump.

'He's dead,' she screamed, the words echoing through the mike across the bungalow lawns. They had the effect of a gunshot. Suddenly, all hell broke loose. People started running in every direction, children began crying loudly, mothers started calling out to their bais. Balloons started popping, trampled under the feet of the crowd. The loud pops of the balloons added noise and fear to the chaos. Around Virkar, the safari-suits reacted like a confused herd that has suddenly lost its leader. They rushed towards the stage en masse, forgetting Virkar's presence. Out of the corner of his eye, Virkar saw Raashi break out of the crowd and run towards the stage. She had a handycam in her hands. Standing on the stage, Raashi swept the handycam over the entire area, shooting the chaos. She was making sure that she captured almost all the guests in an attempt to record everyone who was at the scene of the crime.

Although Virkar was very tempted to join the safari-suits on the stage and participate in their futile attempt to revive Vasant Dixit, he thought better of it. Taking care not to attract any attention, he stood in a corner. His eyes darted over the lawns, trying to take in every minute detail. He tried to focus on anything that looked out of place in the melee, but there was just too much going on. Suddenly, a few of the safari-suits on the stage remembered his presence. From their animated gestures and fingers pointed in his direction, Virkar suddenly realized that they were desperate to find a scapegoat and they had identified him to be the ideal candidate. Virkar slid back towards the bushes that lined the boundary wall and squeezed himself into a small gap between the foliage and the wall. Then he slid along the gap, making his way away from the gate instead of towards it. Virkar had realized that the safari-suits looking for him would go rushing through the gate and run down the open road along the beach, so instead, he decided to go up the hill and down the other side.

As he made his way along the boundary wall, he suddenly found himself outside a small wooden door that was set into the wall itself. Virkar pushed at the door and found it open. Quickly passing through it, he found himself on a path that led uphill towards the main road. Virkar figured that this must be a path used by the local helpers who trudged to and fro from the fishing villages that lay further down the road to the other side of Madh Island. He rushed up the path and through the wooded area.

As he ran, his eyes spotted something colourful through the leaves ahead of him. He immediately stopped and hid behind a tree. A few seconds later, the colourful object broke out of the vegetation and started running up the path away from him. It was a man dressed in a clown's outfit. But he didn't have the clown mask covering his face anymore. In the fraction of a second that the clown had burst from the trees and on to the path, his unmasked face had turned in Virkar's direction. After having spent so much time studying pictures of that face, Virkar had no trouble identifying it. It was Hari Prasad.

47

They ran up the path through the wooded area. Hari Prasad realized that there was no shaking Virkar. He broke through the trees and ran on to the main road, but instead of turning and running up or down the road, Hari Prasad cut across it and plunged into the wooded area on the other side. He continued running downhill and towards the creek that lay ahead, away from the bungalows. In a last-ditch effort, he veered off the path and jumped into the mangroves that bordered the wooded area leading up to the creek. Behind him, Virkar did not hesitate for a second before following suit. Hari Prasad pushed deeper into the mangroves, his feet dragging in the slush, sinking in deeper and deeper till the black, foul-smelling marsh had reached his waist.

Behind him Virkar called out, 'Hari Prasad, there's no point, you can't go further. Give up now.' But Hari Prasad was in no mood to comply. He waded further in till the marsh was nothing but a black liquid. It was the water of the creek flowing past and diluting the marsh. Ahead of him lay the creek he would have to swim across to make it to the saltpans that lay beyond. All of a sudden, Hari Prasad stopped. Behind him, Virkar was gaining. Hari Prasad turned and cast a glance at Virkar's progress. Virkar caught the expression in his eyes. It was fear; the abject, irrational fear that people who can't swim experience when immersed in water.

The man who killed five people in cold blood is scared... He is human, after all, thought Virkar, as he came within striking distance of the man. In response, Hari Prasad plunged into the flowing water only to begin gasping for breath as his feet treaded water and his head was submerged by the black fluid. As the current pulled Hari Prasad away, Virkar swam swiftly towards his thrashing body. In a matter of seconds, Virkar was right behind Hari Prasad. In an expert move, Virkar snaked his arm under Hari's jaw from behind and locked his arm around his neck. Kicking his legs up under the water Virkar used his free arm to cut the water in an expert backstroke. Hari Prasad thrashed his legs in the water but his upper body was immobilized in Virkar's grasp. Virkar dragged Hari Prasad through the current towards the closest piece of land—the saltpans lying across the creek. In a few minutes, he touched dry land. He hauled himself on to the salt-laden hard ground and dragged Hari Prasad behind him, holding him by the scruff of his clown suit. Exhausted, he sat down; beside him, Hari Prasad, too, heaved in deep breaths. A couple of minutes later, their breaths stabilized.

Virkar looked at Hari Prasad, who stared back at him. 'How did you kill him?' he asked after a pause. For a few seconds, Hari Prasad did not say anything. Then he shrugged. 'Helium gas from the balloons.' It suddenly dawned on Virkar that helium gas when inhaled causes the vocal cords to emit a high-pitched sound that is similar to Donald Duck's voice. The first balloon full of helium bursting over his head had caused Vasant Dixit's voice to turn squeaky as he sang the 'Happy Birthday' song. The two life-sized balloons bursting right next to him had released helium at high pressure, asphyxiating him on the spot and creating stroke-like symptoms that finally caused death. As if reading Virkar's mind, Hari Prasad said, 'I wanted him to feel exactly how Tracy didi would have felt when she died while being choked by him.'

Virkar looked into Hari Prasad's eyes and saw that there was no remorse there, only something resembling satisfaction. Virkar finally asked the question that had been troubling him ever since the case had begun: 'Why did you give the compass box clues when your murders were perfect enough for you to get away scot-free? Hari Prasad just shrugged as he said, 'Isn't it clear, Inspector Virkar? I was never afraid of getting caught. I was just afraid that the murders would not catch anyone's attention, like Tracy didi's murder didn't. I didn't want my revenge to be brushed under the carpet and forgotten.'

As Virkar confronted the motives of the Compass Box Killer, he was very tempted to abandon his ethical code and embrace empathy. Ultimately, morality got better of him. He turned a steely eye on to Hari Prasad and said, 'What was the point of taking revenge? You could have lived your life free and clean after prison.'

Hurt and anger flashed in Hari Prasad's eyes. 'You think I didn't try? All through my sentence in prison, I educated myself in chemistry and Ayurveda. I wanted to do further research. But you know what they made me do. They forced me to use my research for wrong purposes. It was then I realized that I was trapped. My life had ended the day Tracy didi's life had. She was like a mother to me, an orphan, who had no one to call his own in this world. She...she did so much for me.' Hari Prasad wiped his eyes and continued, 'It was then I decided that I just wanted to take away the lives of those who took ours.'

Virkar didn't say anything; instead, he stood up and dragged Hari Prasad up to a standing position with him. 'Let's go,' he said in a curt tone.

Hari hesitated and then said, 'I have something for you, Inspector.'

'What?' Virkar raised a suspicious eyebrow. Hari Prasad reached into the pocket of his soaking-wet baggy clown pants and drew out a small revolver. Virkar froze as Hari Prasad opened the bullet chamber and showed him that it was loaded. But then he handed the revolver over to Virkar, who relaxed.

'There is something else,' said Hari Prasad. He put his hand into the other pocket and drew out an old metal compass box from it. Before Virkar could say anything, Hari Prasad handed it to him as well. Virkar looked unsure. Hari Prasad pointed at the compass box and said, 'Aren't you going to open it?'

'What's inside?' Virkar asked.

'The name of my last victim.'

Virkar's throat went dry. He used the tips of his finger to pry open the compass box and, as usual, found a folded note inside. Without displaying any overt hurriedness, Virkar unfolded the note and in the familiar blood writing, read the name, 'Hari Prasad'. Virkar looked up, shocked. For the first time, he understood that Hari Prasad was not going to be caught alive. He wanted to die.

Suddenly, he heard a shout behind him. Virkar swivelled around to see Raashi standing across the creek at the edge of the mangroves. She was pointing the handycam towards them, shouting at Virkar to get out of the way so she could get a clearer shot of Hari Prasad. He was amazed that she had followed them all the way here without him being aware of it. Virkar turned around towards Hari and saw that he had started to run away from him across the saltpans. Virkar aimed the revolver at the fleeing Hari but hesitated, his finger lingering on the trigger.

Behind him, he could hear Raashi shouting, 'Shoot! Shoot!' Just as it looked like he was about to pull the trigger, Virkar spun around again and shot directly towards Raashi. The bullet smashed against the lens of the camera which broke into pieces, destroying every bit of footage that was captured on it. Raashi struggled to maintain her balance but couldn't. She slipped and slid into the soft slush around the mangroves. Virkar then hoisted his arm and threw the revolver into the slush; it plunked into the black water flowing in the creek separating them. With disgust written all over his face, Virkar cast one last glance at Raashi's slush-covered figure. She stared back at him, stunned.

Virkar turned back to look at Hari Prasad who was standing at a distance, watching the scene. For a few moments, both Virkar and he eyed each other without saying a word. Then Hari Prasad turned and ran.

Virkar watched as Hari Prasad escaped. He only looked away when Hari was nothing but a black speck against the white salt mounds in the distance.

Epilogue

Official Report

Based upon the complaint filed by Ms Raashi Hunerwal in the matter pertaining to the killing of Mr Vasant Dixit at his home in Madh Island, Mumbai, a one-man judicial inquiry committee was appointed by the Ministry of Home Affairs, Government of Maharashtra, to examine and investigate the circumstances surrounding Mr Vasant Dixit's sudden death and the involvement of Police Inspector Ramesh Virkar in the matter.

The following facts were found after the cross-examination of various witnesses present at the spot where the incident occurred. Also, results of the departmental inquiry ordered by Additional Commissioner of Police Abhinav Kumar and ACP Crime (South Zone) Wagh have been taken into account.

Findings:

1. Inspector Ramesh Virkar was present at the location under the guise of tendering an apology for an earlier misdemeanour; however, his express duty, as assigned to him by Additional

Commissioner of Police Abhinav Kumar, was to extract a confession to the murder of Ms Tracy Barton, a UK national who was killed in Khandala in 2004. It is believed that it is because of Ms Barton's unsolved murder that Hari Prasad, otherwise known as the Compass Box Killer, initiated his killing spree.

2. Inspector Ramesh Virkar was successful in extracting a confession from Mr Vasant Dixit. This was recorded using latest microchip transmitter technology with a receiver that was on board a civilian fishing vessel, namely the 'Koli Queen', contracted by Inspector Virkar for this job.

3. Inspector Virkar was on his way out from the premises when Mr Vasant Dixit was killed due to inhalation of a massive dose of helium gas (nitrous oxide). This was a result of the helium-filled balloons next to him suddenly bursting. At the time the mishap occurred, Inspector Virkar was at a distance of 300 yards from Mr Dixit and could not come to his immediate aid.

4. After the incident occurred, Inspector Virkar caught sight of the prime suspect in the Compass Box killings, the person known as Hari Prasad. The suspect was, at that time, exiting from a side door at the grounds.

5. Inspector Virkar gave chase to the said suspect, Hari Prasad, following him into the wooded area behind the Dixit bungalow. After having reached an open area behind the woods, Inspector Virkar came close to apprehending Hari Prasad. Whereupon, Hari Prasad brought out a revolver he had been hiding on his person and fired a shot at Inspector Virkar.

6. Inspector Virkar took evasive action to protect himself by ducking aside, whereupon the bullet went past him and hit the camera carried by Ms Raashi Hunerwal, who was also chasing the said suspect, Hari Prasad.

7. Inspector Virkar could only resume the chase after making sure that Ms Raashi Hunerwal was not grievously injured. But by the time he could confirm that she was not hurt at all, the said suspect, Hari Prasad, was out of sight.
8. Despite a lengthy search, Hari Prasad was not found in the vicinity.

The committee dismisses Ms Raashi Hunerwal's claim that Inspector Ramesh Virkar fired a shot towards her which destroyed her camera beyond repair and led to the escape of the said suspect, Hari Prasad, aka the Compass Box Killer. Inspector Virkar was not in possession of a firearm, otherwise he would have fired back at Hari Prasad.

Recommendations:

The committee recommends that Inspector Ramesh Virkar be reinstated to his full service duties for displaying presence of mind in uncovering a long-unsolved case of murder and consequent cover-up as well as for showing exemplary courage in his quest to apprehend a dangerous criminal.

The committee also severely reprimands Ms Raashi Hunerwal, whose presence at the incident spot resulted in the escape of the said suspect, Hari Prasad, aka the Compass Box Killer. It also gives her a strong warning to not waste the time of the Court in the future with false claims.

End Note:

It is advised that the hunt for the said suspect, Hari Prasad, aka the Compass Box Killer, be deemed as inconclusive, and that the case may be closed.

Acknowledgements

I am grateful to:

My mother, Shakuntala, for her love and her prayers.

My publisher, Kapish Mehra, for his risk-taking abilities.

My editor, Kausalya Saptharishi, for her dedication to the *Mumbaistan* series.

My copy editor, Prerna Vohra, for her doggedness.

My friends, Ekta Kapoor, Sudhir Mishra, Arunoday Singh, Chitrangada Singh, Neelesh Misra, Geetanjali Kirloskar, Sudeep, Shylaja Chetlur, Ganesh Venkataraman, Raman Lamba, Monika Trivedi, Krishna Hegde, Tehseen Poonawalla, Stardust Gonsalves, Farida Haider, C.S.S. Latha, Atul Kelkar, Prafful Sarda, R. Gurudath, Justin Yesudas, Uday Ninjoor, Sid Coutto, Divya Kumar, Kumaar Rakesh, Vivek R. Singh and Reine Mountford for giving me their precious time, contacts and creativity.

The team at Rupa—Aruna, Maithili, Singh saab, Hina, Ankit, Hohoi, Anshul, Varun, Ashutosh, Sameer, Ramakrishnan, Sriram, Sharon and Rajan for their contributions, big and small.

I also thank the people in the book trade for their support—

At Crossword: Kinjal, Bala, Sonal, Neha, Rozaline, Virat, Naseem, Shanu and Giridhar.

At Landmark: Rajesh, Arun, Natasha, Varsha, Ayaaz, Kotishwaran and Ved Prakash.

At Reliance Timeout: Dipak, Jacob, Mahendran, Christopher, Niyathi, Uday, Aarun and Soumyashree.

At W. H. Smith: Ram, Bhagyashree and Pratwish.

At Om Books: Sanjay and Sanjeevan.

At Oxford: Vijay, Samson and Bernard.

At Flipkart: Kinshu, Rituraj and Mayank.

At Homeshop18: Anuj and Aparna.

At Infibeam: Akash and Manali.

At Indiatimes: Subhanker, Krishna, Abhas and Tejinder.

And all my readers, for making *Mumbaistan* a resounding success.